# Never Second Guess a Lord

## Second Time Brides, Book 1

By
Sky Purington

## ARE YOU SIGNED UP FOR DRAGONBLADE'S BLOG?

You'll get the latest news and information on exclusive giveaways, exclusive excerpts, coming releases, sales, free books, cover reveals and more.

Check out our complete list of authors, too!

No spam, no junk. That's a promise!

### Sign Up Here

www.dragonbladepublishing.com

*Dearest Reader;*

*Thank you for your support of a small press. At Dragonblade Publishing, we strive to bring you the highest quality Historical Romance from some of the best authors in the business. Without your support, there is no 'us', so we sincerely hope you adore these stories and find some new favorite authors along the way.*

*Happy Reading!*

*CEO, Dragonblade Publishing*

Finally free of a cruel and loveless marriage, wealthy widower Lady Prudence Barrington is determined to make her own way without remarrying. What she does not expect upon arriving at her sister's castle in Scotland is crossing paths with a duke whose name she once slandered for his flirtatious ways. Or that her sister intends to make a match of them.

When Jacob, the Duke of Argyll, learns coldhearted Lady Barrington will be visiting MacLauchlin Castle, he is eager to confront her and perhaps make amends. Forgive the rumors she once spread about him. Help her find her way free of whom she became when married to her late husband, then move on. Or so he thinks until he discovers an interesting, passionate woman underneath her uppity façade.

Friendship eventually turns to scandalous desire, but nothing is as easy as it seems. Not when Prudence refuses marriage but succumbs to love for the first time. A love that is soon threatened by a secret that could very well ruin all they find together.

# Chapter One

*Mayfair, England*
*16 November 1815*

LADY PRUDENCE BARRINGTON yet again peered out of her longtime prison bars overlooking Hyde Park and wondered what the future held. How many times had she done this over the years? How often had she stood at this window, seeing less and less? Seeing nothing but darkness ahead with a cruel, careless husband?

"Lady Barrington?"

She closed her eyes to the crisp octave of her maid Agnus' voice before she opened them and nodded once that she would be right down. Selected for both her stern ways and an inability to attract former Lord Barrington, Agnus curtsied and left with the precision of a well-trained soldier.

"Quite right," she whispered to a man no longer here. "You are *former* Lord Barrington now, and my mourning period is officially over."

Rather than spend another blasted moment looking out this window, she yanked on dark gray gloves instead of black and headed downstairs, ignoring the arrogant faces of her late husband's ancestors. Visages she had once revered but now saw as jail keepers. Haughty overseers who judged her at every turn.

As usual, the pinch-faced butler helped her with her coat and opened the front door without a word. At one time, in her doe-eyed naïve youth, she had hoped he might manage a smile or even a friendly word or two, but those days were gone. Honestly, she would have no idea how to respond if he surprised her with one now. Did she even remember how to smile in return?

Rather than opt for a hat for the long ride north, she pulled her fur-lined hood up against the biting wind of late autumn and made her way into the waiting coach. Expressionless as always, Agnus sat across from her, and they were on their way. Not surprisingly, her maid's features were especially tight today. While typically Prudence would not bother, something about knowing she was leaving this place prompted her to be more cordial than usual.

"It is good of you to stay on with me, Agnus." She tried for a thankful expression, but it felt forced at best. "I hear Scotland is…." *Frigid? Ghastly during the winter? Possessed by questionable people?* "Is hospitable enough."

She had never been to Scotland and, up until recently, was of the mind she never would. Despite having met a few Scotsmen along the way, two of whom behaved well enough, the third one's actions were quite too familiar for her taste. Worse still, he was married, so he should have been above such horrid behavior. A Lord of Rothesay turned Duke of Argyll if she recalled correctly, who was a flirtatious beast much like her late husband.

If possible, Agnus' back stiffened even further. "Scotland is anything but hospitable, and well you know it, my lady."

In addition to her maid's other lackluster qualities, Prudence had chosen Agnus for her blunt ways, so she was not put off by her forthright response. She preferred it to the simpering behavior of her former maids. "I know no such thing." She reminded Agnus of the letter her sister had sent. "According to Maude, MacLauchlin Castle is quite lovely. We should enjoy a pleasant stay."

"If it were but a stay, we may or may not get through it."

Agnus' brow jerked up. "But it is not merely a stay, is it?"

"Time will tell." She turned her attention to Mayfair passing by rather than continuing the conversation. Not that she expected it to be a lively debate anyway. Neither had much use for Scotland, but at least it was not here. Not part of a place that had once possessed so much appeal but now held the opposite.

*"You must come and stay with me,"* Maude had insisted in her letter. *"You will adore Blake and his people."* Prudence could almost see her sister grinning as she wrote, *"We will find you a proper husband to replace the lout you decided to marry the first time."*

Prudence was unsure what put her off more: the fact her sister did not use her husband's proper title or her boorish familiarity with the late Lord Barrington. Either way, she had sighed and continued reading the remaining ten pages, somewhat shocked by their brevity. Maude was notoriously long-winded and could have just as easily written twenty.

She had promptly written back, thanking her sister for the invitation from her and Lord MacLauchlin to come to visit. She had put emphasis on the word *visit* for good measure, as she could not imagine staying there.

But then, she could not fathom returning to Mayfair either.

*"While I appreciate your offer to find me a husband,"* Prudence had replied, scowling all the while, *"I have been left well enough off that I have no need of one."*

She had been, too. Well enough that she could settle somewhere quiet where disagreeable faces no longer looked down from paintings. Where she could navigate her home without an overbearing husband watching her every move.

Oh, such freedom it would be.

No more sitting by quietly as he decided what invitations she could or could not accept. No more being counseled by him at every turn on how she should present herself. The people to whom she should speak. Those she should tilt her nose up at. Best of all, though, no more dreading the rare times he visited her bed chambers only to watch her closely afterward.

Would she, at last, bear him a son? Or had she failed yet again?

Prudence rested her head back and closed her eyes against old heartache. Against the pain she had once felt when she realized bearing children did not come easily to her. Sadness that had dulled over the years until she felt nothing. Until his harsh words about it no longer mattered.

"My lady," came Agnus' monotone voice. "We have just crossed into Scotland and have stopped to take some air."

She jolted awake, startled. Had she drifted off? *Clearly*. So said the late day sun when she took the footman's hand and stepped out of the carriage into even brisker air than before. So this was where Rothesay the Scoundrel was from, as she had taken to calling him over the years. A land not nearly as cultured as England, in her opinion.

"I was hoping we might have a bite to eat, but the driver insists we press on." Somehow Agnus' tight bun seemed to grow stiffer in the whipping wind instead of flying loose. "Probably best in this God-awful weather."

"Indeed." Not that she would admit it, but she rather liked the gusty fresh air. It smelled of pine and sea salt rather than horse manure and perfume. "It is good we brought warm clothing."

"Quite questionable if they will be warm enough." Agnus wrapped her jacket more tightly. Her blade of a nose twitched. "I must say, the scent here is *most* disagreeable."

Rather than respond, Prudence took in the woodland, recalling a time when she had been determined to flee this sort of thing. When she dreamt of leaving the English forests of her youth behind so she could make her grand debut in London. Be the talk of the town. Land a suitor that would give her the status for which she so longed. Little did she anticipate she would land an earl.

One who was a downright monster.

It was something she tried not to dwell on as they continued north a short time later. All of that was behind her now. The future lay ahead. Freedom. A new beginning. A life she would carve out on her own. One that still practiced the propriety to which she had become accustomed, minus a gatekeeper. Without lecherous eyes constantly tracking her whereabouts.

"Oh, dear *heavens*," Agnus muttered when they started down a long, heavily wooded, winding drive barely broad enough to fit a carriage. "One might think we are traveling back to the dark ages. Back to a time when…." Her maid's eyes widened at the looming castle alongside them breaking through the pines and silver birches. "Do you *see* that, my lady? Do you…" Her mouth snapped shut into a hard line before her tone turned ever more disapproving. "It is positively *medieval*."

As they left the tree cover behind and things brightened, Prudence took in the sturdy but sizeable weatherworn castle that had belonged to Clan MacLauchlin for over five hundred years. While not elegant like the English castles she was used to, it possessed a certain stalwart nature she appreciated. From its ancient drawbridge to its turrets and towers, it bespoke a sense of unfailing perseverance. Parts of it had been refurbished, but the main structure remained, standing proudly against the ages, as seasoned and as strongly standing as Prudence had become over the years.

"We must not linger here long." Agnus shook her head and frowned out the window. "This is no place for you, my lady."

"Perhaps not." It might be a castle out of another time, but there was no missing the wealth attached to it as they pulled into the courtyard. "Yet I have been invited, so I must attend."

Verdant hedges were abundant and well-trimmed. Stately outdoor statues were clearly expensive antiques, and the elegant stairs out front were a work of art. A stunning Phaeton carriage was parked nearby with a sturdy well-bred set of black horses, and the coachmen and footmen heading their way were finely presented.

The MacLauchlins had done well over the centuries, gaining

not just wealth and land but substantial titles in both England and Scotland. Truth be told, Maude marrying not just a viscount, but the overseer of this castle was more than Prudence had ever dared hope. After all, her sister's parents had been commoners. Her mother, however, had married a baron after Maude's father passed away, giving Prudence and their other two siblings a much better chance in society.

Almost the moment she thought of her, Maude appeared at the top of the stairs leading to the front door, clasped her hands in delight, then raced down to the carriage when it stopped. While some considered her plain, Prudence had always thought Maude rather fetching with her crop of wild, brown curls and lively cinnamon-colored eyes.

Her personality was another thing altogether.

"At *last.*" Maude cared nothing for decorum but shooed away the footmen, flung the door open, stuck her head in the carriage, and widened her merry eyes at Prudence. "Dear sister, how I have missed you!"

Having forgotten just how lively and unorthodox this sister could be, Prudence stuttered and huffed a little when Maude plunked down next to her, grasped her hand, and looked at her expectantly. "How was your ride? Did all go well? Did you come across any interesting people?" Not waiting for an answer, she smiled at Agnus, who had paled at Maude's boisterous behavior. "Wishing you a warm welcome." Her attention returned to Prudence. "Oh, I *do* so hope the commute went well. It is so very chilly and, oh, the wind! I hope that—"

"The ride went very well, thank you." It may be rude to cut someone off mid-sentence, but Maude might never come up for air if Prudence did not. "Thank you for having us."

"But of course." Beaming all the while, Maude waved it off. "We are sisters, so my home is your home." She looked Prudence over, squeezed her hand, and released a gusty sigh of pleasure. "You look every bit as lovely as you did when last I saw you all those years ago." Her gaze lingered on her face as though she expected to see one thing but saw something unexpected instead. Her smile faltered ever-so-slightly. "But not quite the same." Her voice gentled, and her eyebrows pulled together. "No, not quite the same at all."

"I *did* lose a husband," Prudence reminded her sister, "and it was very difficult."

Or so she told the world. So she showed all who watched and wondered if she would mourn the beast. If she were really as proper as she presented herself to be.

"You did, and I am so very sorry." Maude teared up and embraced her. "So very, very sorry."

She was not sorry in the least, and they both knew it. Maude had disliked her husband from the start and was never shy about it. Sadly, her take on Barrington had been spot on, but pride and a long-developed new take on life kept Prudence from admitting it.

Instead, she stiffened and pulled away.

"It has been a long day, and I wish to rest." She gestured at Agnus and played the proper role. One her servant preferred. "My maid would like to be acclimated with your household and shown her quarters."

Obviously unsure of what to make of things, Maude's eyebrows perked then lowered as she looked between Prudence and Agnus. When her merry-turned-worried gaze landed squarely on Prudence again, she knew her sister would be offering her opinion on the matter soon enough, so she wasn't surprised when she wasted no time broaching the matter when she led her up the stairs to the front door minutes later.

"Are you well?" She linked arms with Prudence. "For you are not the sister I remember, nor do you surround yourself with the sort you once did."

*If she only knew.* "And what sort is that?"

"The sort that is everything you once were." Maude was not discreet but was as open as she had ever been. "Vivacious. Loving. A true adventurer determined to marry well but to never forget who you were. Never forget where you began."

Where she began? "I began titled, destined to marry someone equally titled or above my station."

"Yes, most definitely." Maude shrugged and shot her another concerned look. "But never said so haughtily or with so much detachment."

Had she sounded haughty? Detached?

"I am sure I do not know what you mean." She ignored the butler, who held the door open and greeted her cheerfully with a brogue so thick she barely understood him. "I am as I was when last we met, sister."

"You are no such thing." Maude kept her arm wrapped with Prudence's upon entering. "But we will get to that soon enough." Although her expression was tainted by a pinched brow of concern, she managed another one of her infamous beaming smiles and gestured at the spacious great hall. "Welcome to my home. I cannot tell you how happy Blake and I are to have you here."

A more welcoming and grand space than she'd anticipated, it smelled of freshly baked bread and faint wood smoke from the crackling fire.

"I am so grateful to you both for having me." Prudence kept her tone cordial, sure to address the viscount correctly as they strolled through the hall to a sizable drawing room. "I look forward to meeting Lord MacLauchlin."

"And he, you."

Much to Prudence's mortification, Maude actually *thanked* the servant who delivered a tray of refreshments, then even went so far as to offer said servant an *hors d'oeuvre* before he returned to the kitchens.

"Have you learned nothing, Maude?" she muttered sharply under her breath. "I understand you were lowborn, but you should know better by now, having married so well."

She had married well, indeed, too, according to her tastefully decorated surroundings. The castle might be old, but its interior reflected a fine eye for décor, from the mammoth, exquisitely crafted tapestries to the heavy well-polished, ornate mahogany furniture.

"For shame, Prudence." Maude's countenance donned a seldom-seen seriousness. "The sister I once knew would have offered her servant a bit to eat as well. Would have shown kindness no matter her station." Her eyes narrowed. "In fact, the sister I once knew would have done such if for no other reason than her own sister had been lowly born, so she would not see such looked down upon."

Had she once thought like that? She supposed she had, in another life. In a reality prior to the one she had suffered for over a decade. She tried to reply that those days were long gone, but nothing came out. Instead, her throat went dry at an unanticipated surge of emotion. Feelings she was sure to squelch straight away.

As though she understood her internal struggle, Maude's disappointment vanished in the blink of an eye, and she offered the sort of smile Prudence had forgotten she missed. One that said, *all was forgiven for now*. Nothing was too difficult to overcome.

"Here." Maude handed her a glass of claret. "It has been a long day of traveling. Refresh yourself and come sit by the fire with me."

"Or better yet," came a booming voice with a brogue. "Come sit with us."

Prudence could admit she was surprised by Viscount MacLauchlin when he strolled in, lifted the back of her hand before she offered it, and dropped a quick press of his lips before issuing a charming smile and gently letting go. Kissed was quite handsome She had expected a ruffian like Rothesay the Scoundrel, but instead, he was decently dressed and quite handsome with a thick crop of dark hair and pleasing facial features.

"She looks surprised by me," Lord MacLauchlin said out of the corner of his mouth to Maude, telling Prudence two things. He intended she hear him, and perhaps he was not nearly as civilized as she had originally thought.

"Oh, she is surprised, my love," Maude assured her husband, yet again shocking Prudence with her lack of formality. "But she will get used to all of us in no time."

It was as if they were all some sort of rebel Scottish clan from the dark ages.

"I do hope so, as there are more of my ilk desperate to make her acquaintance again." Viscount MacLauchlin was so uncouth, he winked at his wife. "Someone who did not believe me when I told him she would be our houseguest for a day, let alone longer."

*Our?* As if his castle and all its belongings were every bit as much Maude's. Had she ever heard a man speak that way to his wife? Given her that sort of equality?

"And who might that be, husband?" Maude said in a sing-song voice. A tone that meant she was up to no good and, once again, meddling where she should not.

"Someone Prudence met years ago and, by the sounds of it, loathed on the spot." He chuckled and waved over who had just walked through the door. "Someone determined she rethinks the nickname she coined for him. One that became quite prominent in all the wrong circles."

Prudence went weak in the knees at the sight of the tall, broad-shouldered man striding their way. He wore a daunting look of determination she by no means trusted. Wanted nowhere near her. Especially when his sinfully dark eyes locked on her, and her heart fluttered into her throat.

"Whatever do you mean?" she said, mortified her question came out as a weak squeak.

"You know exactly what Lord MacLauchlin means." The Duke of Argyll stopped directly in front of her, a tad too close to be considered proper, and bowed ever-so-slightly. His steady, dangerous gaze never left her face. "According to the whole of London, you once named me Rothesay the Scoundrel."

# Chapter Two

JACOB HAD LONGED for this moment for years. Hoped he would someday come face to face with the woman who had tried to ruin his good name. Who could have very well ruined his marriage, had his late wife not trusted him.

Much to his pleasure, it seemed Lady Barrington remembered him. So said the flash of alarm in her eyes and the flushing of her cheeks when she offered a crisp nod upon being introduced. Potential enemy or not, there was no denying her stark beauty. From her dainty, delicate features to her plush, kissable lips, she could win over any heart if she tried.

Yet trying to win over hearts was something he suspected she had long given up. And her plush lips? A whole lot less kissable when set in the grim line that greeted him despite how hard he imagined she worked at a cordial smile. Or so he assumed, based on the minuscule twitch of the corner of her mouth. But then, it was to be expected, considering he had just called her out on her bad behavior years ago. Made clear she had coined his unfortunate nickname, Rothesay the Scoundrel.

He could tell by the brief frustration in her almond-shaped sky-blue eyes that she was tempted to reiterate her assessment of him but held back for the sake of propriety.

More so for the sake of his new title.

After all, rumor had it Lady Barrington was, if nothing else, appreciative of those who were a cut above the rest, however flirtatious she might have thought them once upon a time.

She curtsied and bowed her head just enough to be appropriate. "You have my deepest apologies, Your Grace."

Ah, an apology…or so he thought.

"As it were, I have no recollection of naming you or anyone else such a thing," she went on without a bat of her long, thick lashes. Her steady gaze was impossible to decipher. "Nevertheless, I hope we can let bygones be bygones."

No such recollection? What game did she play? The whole of England and Scotland knew what she had done. Yet it seemed she was not about to admit it when he had quite hoped she would. That they might clear the air and start anew. Because he *did* want to start anew with her. Move past the high walls she had built around herself.

Walls he recognized.

While he meant to say he was willing to let bygones be bygones because such had been his very intention, he had trouble putting voice to it quite yet. What held his tongue? Why not release her of any accountability at this very moment? *For that very reason,* he imagined his late wife, Elizabeth, saying. *She must own up to her actions.*

And show a sense of accountability.

How could Lady Barrington ever push past what she had become if she did not acknowledge the harm she had done to others along the way?

"Well, then," Maude said when an awkward silence fell. She looked from her sister to Jacob. "It has been a long day of travel for you both, so I insist you join me and Lord MacLauchlin for a spot of tea."

"I would like that, my lady." He smiled at Maude. "Thank you."

"Our pleasure."

Based on the way Prudence stiffened, he knew that was the last thing she wanted to do, but Maude joined wrapped arms with her and headed for the drawing room, giving her little choice. If that were not enough, she joined her husband on one sofa, allowing Prudence no other option but to sit beside Jacob on the opposite one.

Well aware of their matchmaking ways, he did not miss the knowing look Blake and Maude exchanged. A look he could not help but wonder if Prudence caught. Did she know what her sister was up to? He had figured it out within minutes of arriving when he learned who else was coming. Naturally, Blake hoped Jacob did not mind Lady Barrington being invited as well, given their past. He, of course, had pointed out, "How could I mind when you have already gotten me here under what I suspect were false pretenses?"

Despite the twinkle in his eyes, Blake had denied it. "You two need not cross paths if you wish, but have you not long laid that anger to rest, old chap?"

He had, and his friend knew it.

Now that Blake was in love, he likely wanted Jacob to find that kind of happiness again too. He might have reminded him that no such thing existed beyond what he had shared with Elizabeth. That did not keep him from enjoying the fairer sex, though.

Something he did, albeit discreetly, as tea was served. Despite her rather lackluster, somber clothing, there could be no denying Prudence possessed curves enough to please a man. From her full bosom to the tight cinch of her waist, she would look ravishing in the right gown. He wondered how long she kept her silky chestnut-colored hair. How might it look fanned around her face in the throes of pleasure?

If that is, she was capable of expressing carnal pleasure.

"This is quite the room, Lord MacLauchlin," Prudence said. "I take it these are your ancestors?"

Her assessing yet wary gaze flickered over the medieval Scotsman staring down from the life-sized portrait hanging nearby. She cleared her throat and stiffened to the point he was surprised her back did not break. He wondered what she saw when she looked at it. An ill-kept barbarian with his claymore at the ready? Or perhaps hidden beneath her studious façade, she noticed more? Mayhap the strength of his form?

"Aye, they are my ancestors." Blake grinned at the warrior from whom Prudence had so quickly averted her eyes. "That particular ancestor was laird of this verra castle nearly five hundred years ago."

"Then you have my compliments." Prudence nodded once as though paying him a rare boon. "It is clear your people have come far since then."

Barbarian it was, then.

"*His* people?" Jacob arched an eyebrow at her and tried to ignore her sweet scent, given she had just made clear how she felt about the Scottish. "Once again, you remind me how bold your tongue, Lady Barrington."

Prudence blinked at him as though she had somehow forgotten he was Scottish too. That she had insulted not just the current laird of this castle but a visiting duke. Her gaze whipped back to Blake, yet her hand remained steady on her teacup.

"I meant no harm, Lord MacLauchlin." Prudence did her best to smooth things over. "One could just as easily say my people have come far, too. That the English knights of yesteryear are now civilized gentlemen rather than celebrated conquerors."

"Perhaps celebrated in England," Jacob said dryly. Befriending this lass was going to be harder than he thought. He had no issues with the English and would not start now. He would set history straight, though. "But I think the term 'ruthless' would be a more apt description for such horrific events as the Jacobite Rising and subsequent Highland Clearances, where thousands of Scots lost their lives and clan system no thanks to England's young pretender, Charles Edward." He tilted his head in question. "Would you not agree, Lady Barrington?"

The color drained from her face, yet still, her cup remained steady. Always so steady. Practiced. But was that a telling twitch of her brow? A quickening of her breath?

"I think what Lady Barrington meant to say," Blake said, coming to her rescue, "is that our countries have come far over the centuries. That peace and prosperity are always preferable to war."

"Indeed," Prudence said a little too quickly. "Quite right, my lord." She nodded at Jacob rather briskly. "Your Grace."

"I, for one, am beyond pleased that the past is in the past." Blake kissed the back of Maude's hand and looked at her with unmistakable desire. "Because I could not imagine having anyone by my side other than my beautiful English wife."

The color that had drained from Prudence's face rushed back. Her gaze flashed with embarrassment before she buried what was no doubt going to be a tart remark in a dainty sip of tea. Had no one ever kissed her hand like that? Gazed at her that way?

Ah, yes, *he* had evidently gazed at her like that at one time.

Or so she had claimed.

He credited Blake for handling things so smoothly when he had to be as put off by her offensive words as Jacob. Then again, he well understood the world in which his friend lived right now and how all could be forgiven as long as the lass you loved was by your side. Everything had a way of looking brighter.

"Yes, the past should remain in the past." Maude smiled prettily at Blake before her attention returned to Jacob and Prudence. "Especially considering how wonderful the here and now is bound to be with St. Cecilia's Day nearly here." She clasped her hands in delight. Her eyes grew merry. "As you both know, we will have a variety of musicians visiting MacLauchlin Castle to celebrate, and of course, there will be a festival in town that we *must* attend, for it will be great fun."

While tempted to remind them that the same happened in Argyll and that as laird, he might have remained at his own castle, he was grateful for Blake's deceit. Whilst not directly discussed, his friend knew him well enough to understand he would have wanted to be here for at least a portion of Prudence's stay. Knew he would want to have his moment of reckoning with her, even if it did not go as harshly as some might think she deserved.

"I am sure everything will be very enjoyable." Prudence's features tightened. The color in her cheeks dulled as though the thought of fun, in general, exhausted her. "I fear I grow weary, sister." She set her tea down so precisely on the tray he suspected she would lash out if it sat any other way. "If it would not be a bother, I wish to retire for the evening."

"For the whole evening?" Maude pouted. "But I have such a lovely dinner planned and then games and perhaps a bit of dancing and—"

"And I am sure Lady Barrington appreciates and looks forward to such once she's well rested, my love," Blake interrupted gently. He squeezed Maude's hand in reassurance and looked at Prudence kindly. "Take all the time you need to rest, then we will welcome you properly, Lady Barrington. Until then, there is a chamber awaiting you as well as whatever else you might need to make your stay comfortable."

"You are right, husband." Clearly determined to please her sister no matter what, Maude stood, smiled broadly as only Maude could, and held out her hand to Prudence. "Come, sister. Let me show you to your chambers and see a bath drawn for you."

Truth be told, despite a long day of travel, Prudence smelled nice. Hers was a common perfume used by upper crust ladies nowadays, a scent that, while not unflattering, did not suit her somehow. It seemed too tame and uppity despite, for all intents and purposes, her being exactly that.

"Rest would be most welcome." Prudence remained stiff as she stood without taking her sister's hand and nodded farewell to Blake and Jacob. "Thank you for a pleasant visit, my lord. Your Grace."

Before they had a chance to reply, she marched off with Maude in tow.

The moment she was out of earshot, Blake released an audible sigh of relief and thanked his servant for removing the tea and replacing it with whisky.

"But for the love of my wife," his friend muttered under his breath after dismissing his servants. He poured a glass of whisky for them both. "Beyond her poor opinion of Scots and her tainting your good name, I can see why you so disliked Lady Barrington years ago." He handed Jacob a glass. "To that end, I apologize for inviting you here in the first place."

"You need not apologize." Jacob took a much-needed sip. "We both know I wanted to make her acquaintance again someday." He shook his head. "And I, at least, knew that day would not be easy. Not after so many years of being with that lout to whom she was married."

"So you remain on a crusade to save all those like you once were?" Blake deduced.

"Did you not assume such when you invited me here?" He arched his eyebrows. "And do not claim otherwise."

"I did," Blake admitted. "But perhaps, this was not one of my better decisions."

"Normally, I would tend to agree, but...."

"But what?" Blake said when he trailed off.

"But, however disagreeable Lady Barrington might be, and how destructive she was to my past, I am glad you and your lovely new wife invited me." He was unsure why he felt that so strongly, only that he did. Prudence was every bit as wounded, if not more so, than he had once been. So he tipped his glass to Blake. "I look forward to getting to know both Lady MacLauchlin and Lady Barrington better."

Blake tipped his drink in return. "And I look forward to having you here during the festivities." The corner of his mouth shot up. "More now than ever."

They drank and commenced chatting and catching up before Jacob circled back to what he was curious about. What might help him thaw out the prim and proper Lady Barrington? A task, if he were lucky, that could very well be accomplished by the time he left this castle in a week's time. Then he would move on to his next conquest like he always did.

"I have not been to London in some time," he finally said. "What are they saying about Lady Barrington nowadays? How has her mourning period gone? Did she receive visitors? Visit others?"

"From what I gathered and what Maude knows, she only accepted invitations from a scant few," Blake replied. "The most elite." He shrugged his shoulder. "It is rumored she made very few appearances given how deeply she mourned her late husband."

Jacob snorted and looked skyward. "I doubt even his closest chap mourned his passing." He eyed the way the firelight glittered off the whisky in his glass and frowned. "I think we both can agree few men were as foul as Lord Barrington."

After Prudence had smeared Jacob's good name, he made a point of learning more about both her and her husband.

"Lady Barrington cannot be blamed, husband," Elizabeth had said when he told her what he had discovered. She had crouched in front of him, rested her hand on his knee, and gave him the sort of caring look that made her such a beautiful person. "No more than you could be at one time."

"We *can* agree on Lord Barrington." Blake met his frown. "But perhaps Lady Barrington is best left to find her own way? To spend time with her sister, sister, rather than a duke with good intentions?"

He could tell by the look on Blake's face that he meant to say more but held back.

"What is it, old friend?" he prompted. "If we cannot be honest with each other, who can we be honest with?"

Blake hesitated a moment before he nodded. "You are right." He shook his head and eyed the door Prudence had so recently left through, concerned regardless of what he had said. "Once again, I cannot help but wonder. If she is as lost as you think, should you pursue her, after all?" His gaze returned to Jacob. The corners of his mouth tugged down. "Or would she be better off left to her own devices?" He shrugged. "Perhaps given time and space to find her own way as she seems so determined to do?"

"Does she, then?" Now, this was the sort of information that interested him. "Do tell."

"Well, according to her correspondences with Maude, she seeks to start anew on her own," Blake said. "While Lady Barrington did not say it in so many words, my wife is convinced she never wants to see her home in Mayfair again. That she will never remarry and intends to live out her days alone in her own estate."

It was common enough knowledge that Prudence had borne Barrington no heirs, nor did he have any kin to whom his estate might revert. So this was one of those rare, almost unheard-of cases where everything went solely to his wife.

"Surely she does not mean to live out her days without a husband by her side." He downed his whisky and set the glass down a little harder than intended. "Surely, Barrington did not turn her into…that."

"*That*?" Blake perked a brow at him. "If you mean a lass who is determined to do things on her own terms without a lad telling her how things should be, then, aye, *that* indeed." He shook his head. "Which means a lad, or in this case, a duke, with good intentions who's determined to make her whole again then send her on her way to a bright new marriage might not be best for her."

He arched a brow right back. "Yet you invited me here."

"Yet I did," Blake echoed, blunt. "Because my Maude thinks that, despite what either of you might want, you and Lady Barrington are the perfect match, and true love awaits you."

He chuckled. "Does she think all that?"

"She does."

"Whatever for?" Because he would never love nor marry another after Elizabeth, and he thought he had made that rather plain.

"I wish I knew." Blake polished off his whisky as well. "All I know is she tends to be right about these things."

"Except in this case," he reminded. "Otherwise, you would not have cautioned me against hurting Prudence before throwing her to the wolves."

Blake poured them another. "Well, when you put it like that."

"So I should leave straight away before I break an already-broken heart? One I am utterly certain is firmly encased in ice?"

"As if you could ever escape Maude." Blake chuckled, handed him his glass, and winked. "Though I dare you to give it your best shot."

"So you say." He narrowed his eyes at a friend who knew him all too well. "Yet I sense, despite your denial, that you truly *do* see something in this. Some sort of lasting connection where rest assured, I do not."

"I see no such thing," Blake reiterated. "In truth, I see nothing but broken hearts, in the wake of bringing you and Lady Barrington together." He sipped his whisky and sighed again. "Broken hearts neither of you needs."

What was his friend about? Was he for or against him being here?

"I have been more than clear that I will never love again." He sipped his own whisky, defiant despite himself. "Yet I will linger for a time. See the St. Cecilia's Day festivities through, then be on my way."

The corner of Blake's mouth inched up a mere fraction. "If you wish, Your Grace."

He did. More than ever, now.

"Somehow, you have baited me once more, my friend," he conceded. As it were, his interest was piqued by Blake and Maude's outlook on all this. Why would they ever see him and Prudence as a pair well-matched?

Especially when the troublesome Englishwoman continued being every bit as challenging as he'd imagined she would.

# Chapter Three

"LORD MACLAUCHLIN *BAITED* the Duke of Argyll?" Prudence grimaced and shivered at the sinister feel of it. She frowned at her maid. "Whatever does that mean, Miss Agnus?"

"Mind you, that was a word coined by someone who overheard such, but I would hazard to say it means nothing good at all, my lady." Agnus' mouth pinched so tightly that a faint sunburst of wrinkles blossomed around it. "From what I was able to ascertain from below stairs, Lord and Lady MacLauchlin fancy themselves matchmakers, and you are their latest victim." She pulled Prudence's hair a little too tightly while fashioning it and sniffed in derision. "While yes, a duke is fine and all, let us not forget that he is a *Scot*."

"Quite right." Prudence bit back a flinch when Agnus plunged a decorative comb into her hair. She'd kept to her chambers for the better part of three days, pleading exhaustion, but Maude had claimed she really must attend dinner tonight lest the game caught for her arrival spoiled.

While tempted to argue the game would already be done for, she knew it rude to hole herself away when a duke was in attendance. Even if he were a disagreeable Scotsman. Because he very much was. So said any man of his prestige lowering himself enough to counter a lady beneath his rank about his country's heritage. He should have been above such trivialness and showed his true colors by making her look the fool.

She knew the turbulent history between England and Scotland. Understood that some Scots still held ill will. Who knew it would be royalty, though? Because despite what Agnus said and how Prudence portrayed herself, she was not so cold and uneducated that she did not recognize Scotland had come far. Earned its royals. In fact, there was once a time when she saw herself as no better than any other nationality. That girl might seem a lifetime ago, *was* a lifetime ago, but she had been there, however fleetingly.

"There." Agnus offered a curt nod before stepping back. "That will do, my lady."

She stared at herself in the mirror and barely recognized the woman looking back. While still well within her childbearing years, it seemed sometimes she should see a much older reflection. One that looked like she felt. Gray at the temples. Fine lines on her forehead. An automatic furrow to her brow that would not go away.

Yet something, *someone* else, stared back.

A stern matronly type caught in a visage some might consider young enough to get by. Youthful enough to start over. Did she ever want to be that young again, though? So naïve that nothing mattered but achieving the best marriage possible and bearing her husband a male heir? Then another and another. Mayhap even a girl once his lineage was well-and-truly-secured with boys to claim his rhetorical throne?

"Well done, Miss Agnus." She stood and smoothed her dress. "This will do."

Agnus nodded and spun on her heel, only to stop short at the door when Maude opened it.

She curtsied. "Lady MacLauchlin."

True to form, Maude smiled as though Agnus were every bit her equal. "Miss Agnus."

Her maid nodded and left, giving the sisters privacy.

"Oh, you look just—" Maude's smile faltered when her gaze

landed on Prudence—"just as you did, sister."

Whatever did that mean? She frowned. "How else should I look?"

Maude was rather stunning in a lovely crème colored gown that showed more of her cleavage than necessary.

"Perhaps a little less like you cannot move past your mourning period." As usual, and despite her esteemed position, Maude was as uncouth as ever when she took in Prudence's attire. A functional high-waisted dark grey dress that buttoned straight up the neck, complete with a slightly less gray shawl to soften the look. "Did you not like the dresses I provided for you prior to your arrival? I imagine they would look quite becoming on you."

"Perhaps if I were not just out of mourning because I *am* just out of such, sister, therefore my current attire is expected." While tempted to pinch the bridge of her nose at the instant headache Maude had a way of bringing on, she straightened her shoulders and shook her head. "The dresses you provided were far too vibrant and inappropriate." She clarified the situation. "You have no experience with losing a husband and how one suffers from that kind of loss. No idea what it feels like to be left alone in such…."

"Such what, sister?" Maude prompted when Prudence trailed off, ashamed she had nearly shared more than necessary. Shared what it was like to be caught in a world where one had to mourn a monster. Where even as she did, more monsters lined up, eyeing her for the wealth she might bring them.

"And may I never," Maude said softly, seeing something Prudence had not meant for her to see.

Even so, or perhaps in spite of it, Maude frowned at Prudence's outfit before she swept over to her armoire, whipped open the doors, and pulled out one of the dresses she had provided. "You should positively wear this." Her sister held the lovely golden gown up against Prudence's torso. "It would be stunning on you. The perfect dress for—"

"Dinner." Prudence scowled and stepped away. "Are you not

merely serving food this evening?" She gestured at the inappropriate dress. One she could not envision wearing anymore. "That is far too formal."

"It is no more formal than my dress, and there will likely be dancing in addition to food." Maude sighed. "Please just consider it? You are officially out of mourning now, so you can wear what you like. It would probably do you good and—"

"No." Unwilling to spare the luxurious dress a second glance, she pulled her shawl more securely around her shoulders. "What I have on is just fine, Maude. Please take back your dress or store it away properly."

Maude made to respond with something Prudence suspected worked against that idea but bit her tongue. Instead, shockingly enough, she nodded and returned the dress to the armoire. More surprising still, she made no further comment about Prudence's attire but held out her elbow and requested she join her below stairs.

She could admit her sister had proven quite evolved since last they met. While she would like to credit it to being forced into behaving like a true lady at last, Agnus reported Lord MacLauchlin was not forceful in the least. If anything, the staff claimed he treated his servants like equals. Not just that but, as implied when Prudence first met him, did the same to her sister.

"Surely not," she had said to Agnus. "He must be putting on some sort of airs during his initial months with Maude."

"They claim not." For the first time ever, Agnus seemed at a loss for words. "It is very—" her expression tightened, and she struggled for the right words—"very odd. Even for these people."

"These people being the Scottish who had, as far as she could tell, shown both her and her maid a great deal of courtesy. No small thing considering how Agnus could be when they visited other households. She ran a tight, unforgiving ship when it came to her mistress's needs. Not with kindness, either, but with a stern voice and a sharp, cold look that kept all in line.

So what Agnus reported could be trusted.

A very good thing, given Prudence had spent the past few days wondering how she should go about things. She had never felt so out of her element as she did in this castle. So discomforted, now that she was freed from one cage only to find herself closed off in another.

"Are you though?" Her sister, Grace, would have asked if she were here. "Or have you simply locked yourself away in yet another cage?"

Grace, or Lady Grace Howard, had visited her as often as Prudence's late husband would allow. Where in the early years, she had appreciated it, as time went on and Grace became married, Prudence started to dread it. She had begun to invite Grace less because she cared naught about the mad love her sister felt for her husband nor the fairytale life in which she lived. Invited her less because she cared naught about the mad love she felt for her husband nor the fairytale life in which she lived.

That was neither here nor there now, so she set it from her mind as she and Maude made their way downstairs. The great hall had undergone a transformation over the past few days in preparation for the festivities. More chairs were set about, and musicians came and went, setting up instruments in various rooms.

"Tomorrow is bound to be great fun." Maude smiled and thanked a servant who handed them refreshments at the bottom of the stairs. "Most especially the festival in town." She gave Prudence a rather stern look before she could deny her. "As my guest, I fully expect you to join me. It will be good for you to get some fresh air."

While going to a festival sounded awful, she knew by the firm set of Maude's jaw denying her would be a waste of time.

"Besides," Maude went on despite receiving no argument, "I would like you to get to know my husband better. And, of course, the Duke of Argyll because he is a good family friend." She arched an eyebrow at her as they stopped in front of the great hall fire to allow men carrying a pianoforte to pass. "One who has been asking after you."

"Whatever for?" He was positively the last person Prudence wanted to see. If she had her way, she would have remained in her bedroom until he departed. "I would think he would have very little interest in my whereabouts."

"As would I," Maude agreed a tad too bluntly. "Yet he seems eager to spend more time with you."

She tried not to frown, as it was unbecoming for a lady, but Lord, did she scowl on the inside. That man was infuriating. From the blatant way he had behaved years ago to his argumentative behavior in the drawing room the other day. Now that the word *baited* had been used, she suspected the duke was up to no good. Perhaps eager to settle the score, which spoke much to his character. But then, should she be so surprised?

He was clearly as ill-mannered now as he had been years before.

She might have been polite enough to excuse his behavior by denying she had ever called him "Rothesay the Scoundrel", but she would not be so gracious a second time. Not if he pulled something untoward in order to reap some uncouth revenge. Because truly, all she had nowadays was her good name.

"I cannot imagine why he wishes to spend time with a widower he claims insulted him. I would think his time better spent in London." She tried not to narrow her eyes as she scanned the busy hall for him. "The season is just beginning, and he is in need of a wife, is he not?"

"While some might say yes, I doubt he will ever take one," Maude said softly, catching Prudence off guard with her sudden despair. "How could he when he will only ever love his late wife? Or so they say." Her eyes grew glassy. "Few have found such deep love from what I hear. Such a timeless connection." She shook her head and rested her hand over her heart. "I hear he suffered from deep melancholy after he lost her. That he swore never to remarry."

Leave it to Maude to grow overemotional, however intriguing the topic. Honestly, she found his sentiment hard to believe, considering his flirtatious manner years ago. What game was he playing? It made little sense, given his actions when with a woman he claimed to love so much. While not one to gossip, one thing stood out the most about his supposed heartache.

"I find it hard to believe he does not wish to remarry," she said, "as his late wife did not provide him with an heir, did she?"

"However much he wished it, I fear not." Maude dabbed the corners of her eyes with a dainty handkerchief. "Yet that does not drive him to remarry. No surprise, I suppose, given the duke does not seem all that enamored with his new title or its obligations."

"Goodness." Did he not realize that however atrocious, he could keep on with his womanizing ways despite his title and marriage? Her late husband certainly had. "How odd."

"To say the least." Just like that Maude broke into a smile and whipped out a fan when she spied her husband and the duke heading their way. "But very romantic, yes?"

Romantic? No such thing existed, and her impetuous sister best learn that soon. However enamored Lord MacLauchlin might seem when he kissed Maude on the cheek, then gazed at her so lovingly, it was surely all for show.

The duke offered Prudence what must appear—to most—a warm smile. "So good to see you again, Lady Barrington."

It was no such thing, and he knew it. Still, she curtsied. "Your Grace."

He looked quite the sight in his evening finery. Whether or not she found his sort appalling, she could not fault the appreciative glances he received from women. Between his title and dashing appearance, some might consider him quite the catch. Most would likely find him handsome with his masculine, chiseled features and thick ebony hair. Where she preferred a man with fairer hair and a less intimidating build, she supposed some might be drawn to his broad-shouldered height.

"I hope you have enjoyed your stay so far, Lady Barrington." Lord MacLauchlin tore his gaze away from her sister long enough to be civil. "I encourage you to enjoy everything Castle MacLauchlin has to offer."

"Thank you." She nodded graciously. "I appreciate your hospitality, Lord MacLauchlin."

"Oh, stop being so formal." Maude waved her off. "We are all family here." She grinned at the duke. "Even Jacob. I mean, Your Grace."

"Sister," she snapped, baffled by Maude's behavior. While no great fan of *Jacob's*, as she called him, her lack of decorum was beyond reproach, and Prudence made that clear when she looked at him. "My deepest apologies, Your Grace." How to explain it? "My sister's upbringing was not of the caliber to which you are accustomed."

"Yet it is a caliber that is most welcome in my—*our*— castle, Lady Barrington," Lord MacLauchlin said tightly before he held out his elbow to Maude. "If you will join me, Lady MacLauchlin? I believe we are needed elsewhere." He perked a brow at the duke. "Perhaps, as you are indeed like kin, Your Grace, you would enjoy showing Lady Barrington around Castle MacLauchlin before dinner is served?"

"But, of course, Lord MacLauchlin."

Where she thought for sure Maude would titter on and remain by her side as she would have before, her sister did the opposite. Instead, she gave Prudence a cordial enough smile, linked arms with her husband, and strolled off without another word.

The duke held out the crook of his elbow. "Shall we, then, Lady Barrington?"

If she knew this was how things were going to go, she would never have left her room. Not for all the wealth and prestige in the world. Yet curious eyes were watching, so she had little choice but to accept his offer and slip her arm into his. To allow who had been the sole focus of her hatred at one time to escort her along as though being on his arm was an honor.

*"Because it is an honor," Grace would say. "You said as much years*

*ago, too, if you recall? You remember. In the drawing room over tea when we spoke of all the esteemed acquaintances you were making because of your elevation in society. I do believe the Rothesays were among them. That in time, Lord Rothesay and his wife might very well have become a duke and duchess, so you were eager to make their acquaintance."*

And now here he was, a duke, and she on his arm. The only problem was everything in between. How he had treated his wife despite what Maude said. The harm he must have caused her with his flirting. His inevitable infidelity. How heartbroken she must have been.

"You need not show me around, Your Grace." Her voice sounded tight even to her own ears, but it could not be helped. "I realize, given the false impression you are under, that it might be an unsavory task."

If she could dismiss herself and flee back upstairs, she would, but that would seem rude at this juncture. She had made an appearance, and as sister to the Lady of the Castle, she must see things through.

Especially given who escorted her.

"I will admit it would be less of an unsavory task if you did not appear so unhappy," the duke said softly enough to spare her from others overhearing. He steered her down a less busy hallway of candle-lit chandeliers and old paintings. "Do I truly upset you so?"

"Of course not." What else to say to a duke? *Yes, I think your actions years ago were reprehensible. How* dare *you?* "I was merely put off by my sister's rude behavior."

She tried not to look at the towering Scots staring down from even older portraits. Feared seeing the same harsh, judgmental looks in their eyes as those she had left behind in Mayfair. She also tried to ignore the Scotsman on her arm. How petite she felt beside him. How strong his presence seemed. What was that pleasant scent he wore? A bit of a spicy masculine aroma.

"Yet I was not put off by your sister's behavior," the duke

made clear, drawing her attention back to the conversation. "If anything, I quite appreciated it."

"Did you?" She tried to smooth away a frown when she glanced at him. "Whatever for?"

"For the kinship of it." Though he smiled cordially at those who curtsied in passing, she heard the strain in his voice when he confirmed what Maude had said. "You see, I never wanted to be a duke. Would have much preferred a lesser title and people around me who did not feel the need to bow at every turn. Who might, like your sister, address me by my given name."

*Surely not.* "So you wish you were a commoner?"

"At times," he admitted. "Yet I know I can affect more change as I am now."

*What an odd thing to say.* "What kind of change?"

"Any change that is for the better," he said. "Poverty and unemployment in the lower classes, for starters." His gaze drifted over the wealthy furnishings around them and the finely dressed people passing. "While it might seem a time of prosperity for those of us walking halls such as this, others suffer. Those who keep both Scotland and England afloat with their hard work."

She might have expected having any number of conversations with him, but not this. Surely, he jested. Why, though? Why lie about such a thing? It seemed cruel even for him.

"I wish to return to the great hall." Duke or not, she let go of his arm, spun on her heel, and started back the way they had come, only for a servant to open a door and gesture inside. "If you would, my lady and Your Grace. They bring a special pianoforte down the hall, and we cannot risk it being nicked or dropped. The way must be cleared."

How many new pianos were her sister and Lord MacLauchlin bringing in? She could tell by the serious look on the servant's face this was quite the affair, so she entered the dimly lit room only to realize there was no one else in there. Rather, when the door clicked shut, she was in the last place she wished to be.

All alone with the Duke of Argyll.

# Chapter Four

J ACOB WAS UNSURE how to feel about the timing of his seclusion with Lady Barrington. While some might think Blake had planned it, he knew his friend would never be so unfeeling.

Not given the piano that was being so carefully carried down the hallway.

The room they ended up in was one of the more intimate ones in the castle, with a small sitting area in front of a fire that, like many hearths over the next few days, had been kept lit. And like most rooms on this floor, there was an array of liquors left out on a side table.

He poured himself a whisky and gestured at her glass. "More while we wait?"

"No, I have plenty," she began, only to seem startled her glass was nearly empty. As though she were surprised to realize she had been sipping quite steadily from it since he joined her in the great hall.

"I insist." He refilled her glass with claret before she could say no, then gestured at the chairs in front of the fire. While he should keep things properly civil, he was in no mood after catching a glimpse of that piano. If anything, he felt more direct than usual. "Now that you cannot escape so quickly, shall we sit until we can leave?"

Her eyebrows drew together. "Pardon me?"

"Shall we sit?"

"You know full well that is not what I referred to." She shook her head and worked against an improper frown. "I was not trying to escape."

"Yes, you were." He rested his hand on the back of one of the chairs. "Sit, Lady Barrington. I insist so that we might speak plainly."

"About what?" She sat, her back more rigid than ever as she eyed him. "I hardly know you, Your Grace, so I cannot see what we have to say to one another."

Biting back a heavy sigh, he sat and sipped his whisky when he would much rather down it in one swig and start on another. "We, more so, *you*, can admit to what you would not when last we spoke." He gestured at their surroundings before leveling his gaze on her lovely, if not defiant, face. "You can, in complete privacy, share why you dishonored my good name years ago."

"I did not."

"You did."

"I tell you, I did not."

"Blast it, you *did*, and I deserve to know why because I did nothing untoward."

When her mouth thinned into a tight line, her cheeks flamed red, and she started to stand, he continued.

"If you tell me, give me that much, I will tell you why everyone is making such a big fuss about the pianoforte coming down the hallway at this very moment." He clenched his jaw and fought sharing this with such a difficult woman, but he did have a mission here. "More than that, I will tell you what it has to do with me."

She started to lower into her chair again but clearly thought better of it. Instead, she set aside her glass, squared her shoulders, and stood with her back to the hearth. Rather than reprimand his cursing, she clasped her hands neatly in front of her, stared down her nose at him, and made things clear.

"My apologies, Your Grace," she said calmly despite the rosiness of her cheeks and the unexpected fire in her thickly lashed eyes, "but you are not my husband, so you will *not* order me about." She shook her head sharply. "This is an inappropriate situation for us both. It puts my good name at risk."

It would if she were a blooming virgin, and this was her coming out. Neither of which was the case. And while tempted to cut back with such, he refrained. Not only because it worked against his goal but because he caught the slight shake of her hands as she clasped them together more tightly.

Her emotions were obviously running as high as his.

"I am sorry," he said softly, meaning it. While determined to get long-awaited answers first, it was clear Prudence was every bit as wounded as he thought she might be. That underneath her thoughtless words of years ago existed a woman struggling to break free of binds. He was pleased, however, to see she *was* struggling. Fighting. That Barrington had by no means broken her.

So he decided to go about this differently.

"The pianoforte is my late wife, Elizabeth's." He sipped his whisky and turned his gaze to the flames, remembering how she had looked playing it. The way her fingers had flown over the keys. "She has MacLauchlin blood, so her most favored instrument belongs back with her beloved clan."

Blake had initially denied Jacob when he said it was finally time for it to come home but had, at last, given in. Understood that, in some small way, he needed this. That despite moving on enough to help others, he still suffered himself and seeing it day after day had grown too difficult.

Silence hung heavy for several long moments before Prudence finally spoke.

"I am sorry as well," she said just as softly before clearing her throat. "I had no idea you were married to a MacLauchlin. It was kind…and right of you to bring it back here." However stiffly, she returned to her chair, folded her hands on her lap, and seemed to weigh her words. Finally edged toward the disservice she had done him years before. "Why did you do it, then? Why show such untoward affection so openly with me years ago if you loved your wife so much? Because if you did such with me, you surely did so with others."

He was not sure where to begin with her accusation. Untoward affection? When? In that brief interlude in Hyde Park, surrounded by friends? During the few minutes they were introduced, then went their separate ways?

"I did *no* such thing," he said more vehemently than intended. "I would have never betrayed my wife like that. I would have sooner died."

"You did, though." She swallowed hard. "I saw the look in your eyes when you took my hand. Saw the way you wanted to kiss it. How your gaze roamed my face with appreciation despite having a lovely, devoted wife. How you thought nothing of saying you would like to call on me and—"

"Your Grace?" Blake's butler said when he opened the door, interrupting the moment. "The pianoforte has been returned to where Lady Rothesay would have wanted it. Where you wanted it."

"Thank you." While a part of him wanted to head there straight away, and another wanted to run in the opposite direction, he knew the best place, the only place, had to be here until he and Prudence had settled things. "Please close the door behind you."

Rather than drink anymore for fear of lashing out when he needed to remain calm, he set aside his whisky and turned his attention to Prudence. Turned to a woman who was, without doubt, every bit as lost as he once was.

"I remember our brief encounter as well, Lady Barrington," he said. "However, I recall it a tad differently than you. Would you like to hear how I remember it?"

She clenched her hands so firmly that her knuckles turned white. "If you insist."

He kept from grinding his teeth. "I am not insisting but asking."

Her tone was unrelenting. Distrustful. Not apologetic in the least. "Then do go on."

Unwilling to look at her when he spoke of this because she had, after all, nearly turned it into something it was not, he focused on the fire once more.

"The day in question happened to be mine and Elizabeth's fifth wedding anniversary," he said. "And she was arriving at Hyde Park for a picnic soon after you and I first met. It was all planned. A special picnic to celebrate her. Us. The love we had found together."

"Then how could you—"

"What?" He frowned at Prudence, remembering well how horribly stern she had looked that day. Vividly recalled what it had felt like to feel that way. He heard the stories about her husband. Knew what kind of man he was. What he could not have foreseen was the viper he had turned his little wife into. "How could I have shown you kindness? Smiled at you? Taken your hand?"

"You asked to call on me," she exclaimed.

"I asked if my *wife* and I might call on you and Lord Barrington," he corrected. "Nothing more."

Her finely arched eyebrows snapped together. "Why would you do that?"

"Do what?"

"Wish to call on my late husband and me?"

"Because that was what was done." Her confusion saddened him, but he understood. She really had no idea. "Because I thought you would get on well with Elizabeth." He shook his head. "It was nothing more, Lady Barrington. I loved my wife dearly. Ask anyone."

"I did." She blinked at him. "I asked…"

"Who?" He persisted when she trailed off.

"People I trusted," she assured. "People who would know the truth of things."

Meaning those who simpered at her heels and gossiped in her wake. Those who had most certainly enjoyed spreading something as scandalous as Rothesay the Scoundrel around town out of nothing more than boredom.

"Perhaps you want to give more thought to what actually happened that day, my lady," he said after a time, his temper in check because Elizabeth had made him see this years ago. Helped him understand that Prudence was as cold-hearted as he once was because she had forgotten how to be anything else.

He finally looked her way. Hoped she saw the truth of things in his eyes. Prayed it did not push her further away, no matter how difficult it was to hear. Hoped it did not embarrass her even though he knew it would. That it probably should.

"I recommend you reflect more on how you perceive things in general," he said, "because what you thought you saw, perhaps even felt, did not happen." He shook his head again. "Not at all." He bit back emotion. "Elizabeth saved me, and I loved her. Loved her more than you can possibly imagine."

While tempted to leave her there alone with her eyes still narrowed, Elizabeth would look poorly on it, so he stood and gestured at the door. "Shall we continue our tour?"

He prayed she said no. Hoped she wanted to return to the great hall and rejoin Maude wherever she might be. Instead, Prudence continued considering him before she finally stood and nodded once. "I would like that."

Like that? Truly? *Why?* Her reasoning, or so it seemed, shocked him when they stepped out the door.

"Perhaps not that way quite yet, Your Grace." Her voice was surprisingly gentle when he looked down the hall in the direction they had carried Elizabeth's piano. "There is more to see here at MacLauchlin Castle back the way we came, is there not?"

There was, and however stern Prudence resumed being when she slid her arm into his, he appreciated the flicker of compassion in her voice. The hint of a heart beneath all the coldness. Did that mean she believed what he had said? Impossible to know because she returned to being properly prudish when he led her through various rooms and explained the castle's history as Elizabeth once had to him.

In fact, Prudence was the only other lass with whom he had walked through this castle. While there were moments where he again felt Blake had gone too far, bringing him here to confront and perhaps find temporary companionship with her, there were other moments of ease. Comfort if for no other reason than she proved more interesting than anticipated. Or should he say she had far more questions than he foresaw, given the heavy conversation they had left behind? Or perhaps because of it? A means to put distance between herself and the uncomfortable truth of things?

Her questions had nothing to do with his misinterpreted flirting years ago but, thankfully, about the castle and its history. Clan MacLauchlin over the generations. How had they remained in one castle for so long when things were so difficult? How did they hold their ground against her English? And she *did* phrase it that way whether she realized it or not.

"I suppose you could say we Scots were resilient." He led her into a room with more weapons mounted on the walls than pictures. "We tended to want to keep what was ours, to begin with."

"I see," she murmured, gazing at the various blades. Again, she showed a more inquisitive mind than he expected. "And all of these are ancestral weapons?" She looked from a sheathed sword to him. "All blades I assume the MacLauchlins fought us English with?"

"Perhaps or perhaps not." He eyed the blade she had been drawn to. One mounted at eye level. "Sometimes it had nothing to do with one's obvious enemy but another sort of enemy altogether."

"Do tell."

"Well, in the case of this blade, it was a MacLauchlin who realized a foe was not really a foe at all." He removed it from the wall, unsheathed it, and admired the long, lethal metal. "In the end, the laird understood his battle was only ever with himself and not the enemy he treated so harshly." He shook his head ruefully. "So he hung this blade where he could see it best, so he never forgot his folly."

Quick to figure out he was teasing, more so running a parallel to her own assumptions years ago, Prudence made to speak, then snapped her mouth shut before she straightened and managed a proper scowl. "You jest?"

"I do." He could not help but smile. "In truth, this sword was a gift from an allied clan long ago. No doubt a means to settle a dispute."

She arched her brows. "Is it not counterproductive to give a weapon of war to make peace?"

"Not to medieval Scots," he said. "Especially in these parts. Weapons were every bit if not more valued than currency." When he saw her lingering interest in the blade, he gestured at the hilt. "Would you like to hold it?"

"Certainly not," she said, even though he suspected she did. "What interest would I have in holding such a thing?"

"One never knows." He returned the sword to its mount. "Perhaps you simply wanted to hold something that intrigued you?"

"A sword, intrigue me?" She offered a dainty little shiver and continued on but not before glancing at the sword one last time. "What would I want with a blade that belongs in our past?"

"Again, one never knows." They continued strolling from room to room. "Perhaps you enjoy history. And whilst it might have served more purpose in the past, I, for one, enjoy jousting sparring with a sword nowadays."

"Do you?" She perked an eyebrow. "Why?"

While he would typically say for the sport of it, something about the genuine curiosity in her eyes made him want to give her an equally genuine answer. "I suppose if I were to be honest, to release pent-up emotions."

She seemed surprised by that. As though he should not have admitted such. Yet minutes later, as they continued strolling from room to room, she replied. "Did I anger you that much, then?"

"Not anger at you, Lady Barrington." He supposed if there were ever a time to give her some of his history, it would be now. "When I first began sparring, it was anger at everyone in general. Dislike of what I had experienced thus far in life. As time went on, that anger vanished until it returned upon losing my wife."

Prudence was about to reply when a small group of people entered the room and gathered by the hearth to chat. Understanding by the flicker of discomfort on her face that she would rather not have this conversation around others, they started back toward the great hall.

While he would have preferred to remain in her company because he sensed they were making headway, he was forced to leave her in Maude's miraculously available hands upon their return. This might not be his estate, but there were still plenty who wished to speak to him about other matters. Ways in which he might help them. How they might assist him if he were ever in need. So he bid Prudence farewell in hopes they would reunite later that evening.

"She has not gone all that far," Blake said when they crossed paths a short while later. "We shall rejoin them soon enough."

When he looked at his friend curiously, Blake chuckled. "Most might not see it, but it is obvious enough by the way your eye wanders to where Lady Barrington vanished with my Maude that you are eager to run into her again."

"I suppose I am." They headed for the study. "I fully expected one thing upon spending time with her and discovered quite another."

"And what did you discover?"

"That she is—" he did not search long for the right word— "interesting. Worth getting to know better."

He could tell by the dubious look on his friend's face he found that hard to believe, and he did not blame him. Prudence was a difficult woman. But, again, he stood by the premise she was not always that way.

As it happened, Blake relented and proved that theory correct.

"Maude said she was once very different." He shook his head as though he found it hard to believe. "That she was vivacious and happy. She had never been uppity or looked down on others."

"I believe it." And he was not sure why other than he had caught glimpses of a different woman today. It had not been much, but she was there. "I look forward to seeing if that lass still exists." He slid a knowing look MacLauchlin's way. "But I suspect you hoped I might say that despite how disagreeable you might find her."

"Honestly?" Blake shook his head. "Maude did, but yet again, I wondered at it. If such a thing were truly a good idea."

"So the timing of Elizabeth's pianoforte was not planned?"

"It was not." Blake stopped and frowned at him. His brows furrowed. "Surely, you do not think I would be so insensitive?"

"I do not." He clasped Blake's shoulder. "But I had to ask as the timing was most unusual."

When Blake asked him why he told him what had happened.

"So it gave you two an opportunity to connect in a way you did not anticipate, I take it?" Blake narrowed his eyes. "And that made all the difference?"

"Surprisingly, it did." He squeezed his friend's shoulder. "I am convinced your wife is right about what lies beneath her sister's difficult exterior."

"Then perhaps..."

When Blake trailed off, he understood what he did not say. His concern yet again that Jacob might cause more harm than good going forward. That it may, indeed, be best to let Prudence find her own way, no matter how isolated and lonely he sensed it would be.

Yet he knew he could not.

Especially when he laid eyes on her an hour or so later and saw the last thing he wanted to see.

# Chapter Five

I F PRUDENCE COULD race back upstairs like a wallflower desperate to escape, she would, but those days were long gone. Instead, she found herself surrounded by men wishing to speak with her. Eyeing her with far too much appreciation, in her opinion. Were they blind? Did they not see she was past her prime? For goodness sake, she was dressed discreetly enough.

"I am so sorry to have left you alone for even a moment," Maude said upon her return. "The head cook needed me." She nodded graciously to the men surrounding Prudence, bid them a lovely evening, and gestured across the way. "Pardon us, gentlemen. Lord MacLauchlin and the Duke of Argyll await us."

"The next time you need to see to the kitchens, please let me know ahead of time," Prudence hissed out of the corner of her mouth. "I was bombarded for lack of a better word."

"I think perhaps you were just admired, sister." Maude's newborn smirk fell beneath Prudence's stern look. "Despite that horrid dress, you really are quite stunning. And out of mourning, lest it slipped your mind."

"I am no such thing," she stuttered. "Stunning, that is." She sighed and shook her head, surprisingly relieved to see Jacob and Lord MacLauchlin heading their way. "What I mean to say is I am only just out of mourning, and opportunists should realize that." She saw things for what they were. "It is clear word has gotten out that I am a wealthy titled widow now."

"Or," Maude countered gently, "they simply see what I do. A beautiful young woman who is out of mourning."

"*Young?*" Was her sister mad? "I am no such thing."

"You are younger than I," Maude reminded.

"Your point?" She worked against an improper frown when she wanted to outright scowl. "As you are quite old, too."

"Perhaps." Maude seemed to be holding back a chuckle as she looked Lord MacLauchlin's way with unabashed affection. "And even so, my husband looks at me with love and desire because he knows this night, like every other, and all moments we try to steal in between, I am still—"

"Stop." Proper decorum or not, this time, she *did* scowl at her sister. "I need not know about your private affairs, Maude. That is one step too far."

Maude's eyebrows shot up. "Even for sisters?"

"Most *especially* for sisters." How could she not see that? Then again, this *was* Maude. "While granted, you are lovely, you must understand any discussion having to do with intimacy is most inappropriate. That is for you and your husband alone." She nodded once and gave her sister a stern look. "Do you understand?"

"I do," Maude said readily enough, yet Prudence did not miss the smirk once again hovering beneath her dutiful façade. "My apologies, dear sister."

Lucky for Maude, because Prudence had a bit more to say about the matter, the Duke of Argyll and Lord MacLauchlin finally joined them. Strangely, just like that, any irritation she might have had with her sister fled when Jacob held out the crook of his elbow to her.

"Might you join me to dine, Lady Barrington?" Scottish brogue and all, his deep, rich voice curled through her in a way it had not before.

She slipped her arm into his. "I would like that, Your Grace."

While she would not exactly call them allies, he had, however odd considering her hatred of him for so long, become a welcome rescuer. So to speak. Anything to keep those foolish men who had flirted with her away.

The truth was Jacob had surprised her when they'd spoken earlier. No, that was not the right word. He had *shocked* her. If she had learned nothing else during her long, lonely years of dealing with her late husband, it was how to spot lies. How to hear how genuine words might be.

As it turned out, the Duke of Argyll was a truthful man.

Moreover, he was a loving man. A creature she had no idea what to make of, but there he had been sitting in front of the fire earlier, telling her things she could never have imagined a man saying about his wife. Never imagined feeling. Because he had, whether he realized it or not. She had seen his eyes grow glassy when he stared at the flames. Heard the pain in his voice.

Knew, without question, he had loved his late wife.

What she could not understand was the discrepancy between what she remembered about her first encounter with him and his viewpoint about how it had actually gone. It made no sense. He had flirted. Made eyes at her.

Or *had* he?

She was certain he had but feared her own mind at that particular point. Her relationship with her late husband, Randolph, had turned especially difficult around then. She had learned things she had not expected about him. So what if she saw something that was not really there during her encounter with Jacob?

Fortunately, she and the duke sat beside each other at dinner, much welcomed not only because she had no interest in fending off more unwanted suitors but because she rather enjoyed chatting with him. As to be expected, he was educated on a great many things, but it was more than that. He lent liveliness to what would normally be hum-drum conversations.

So said the tour he had given her earlier.

She had been riveted the moment he started showing her around. He had a way of drawing one in with how he spoke of his homeland. Made one see Scotland in a whole new light. He told her the story behind nearly every painting. The plight this ancestor or that faced. How trying times were.

He shared so much and with such feeling that she knew this was personal for him. That his late wife had likely given him the same tour. Despite her distrust of love, she could not help but find it in her heart to appreciate that. What would it have been like had her own husband done that for her? Explained his ancestors immortalized in the portraits at Mayfair? Had he looked at them with the same passion and interest as Jacob did of people who were not even blood-related?

Their conversation was no less dull when they sat and ate. The fare was markedly different than what she was used to in England, so he gave her a full account of everything as it was offered to her, then, after it was served, explained why it was such a popular dish in Scotland.

She was rather stunned by how quickly time flew by. It seemed too brief a period before people finished eating and headed off to listen to music and enjoy themselves. Too little time when it had been hours. While no longer hungry, she found herself wishing there was more food to sample, if only to hear Jacob's passion. His vivid interest in just about all things, it seemed.

Or so was the case until piano music drifted into the room. When that happened, the same veil she had seen fall over his features earlier found him once again. A sadness that had everything to do with his late wife's pianoforte.

While she had every intention of bidding him goodnight after they ate, something about the lost look on his face made her speak out of turn. Or perhaps just a need to help him escape a heartache she knew all too well, however different its design. "I could use a spot of fresh air, Your Grace." She looked at him kindly. "I hear there is music to be had outdoors as well. Perhaps you would escort me?"

He looked at her blankly for a moment as though he did not

see her before his gaze seemed to clear. In that brief moment, she saw what she had felt earlier. A need to flee. Only it was his need this time. Not from her. She understood that. But from memories. Heartache.

"If you would not mind, I believe…" he began but trailed off.

However awkward the moment, she understood what he meant to say. "You believe perhaps it is time to retire?"

Where hours before, she might have thought him putting on some sort of show so he could go about his business, now she knew better. The Duke of Argyll was suffering. Needed to be alone. No longer wanted to be around anyone, including her.

And she did not fault him for it nor, ironically, distrust him.

"Then I bid you a goodnight, sir." After she stood, she clenched her hand when tempted to rest it on his shoulder in comfort. "For I, too, am tired." She offered him what she hoped appeared a heartfelt smile because it very much was. "Perhaps I will see you over breakfast?"

"I would like that, Lady Barrington." He stood, nodded, and clenched his hand when she suspected he wanted to take hers. Instead, he lowered his head before his warm gaze returned to her face. "Very much so."

Though disappointed the evening was ending, she knew it was for the best. Her viewpoint of Jacob might have shifted some, but it was better they not spend too much time together.

"Why, sister?" Grace would likely ask, seeing everything from a romantic angle. "Are you afraid your tyrant might not be such a beast after all? That he might deserve love rather than slander?"

Did he deserve love? Quite possibly, considering how much he had clearly cared for his late wife. Slander? She still had no idea. Still had no clue what to make of what she witnessed that day so long ago.

"I trust your evening was manageable, my lady?" Agnus said once she returned to her room. "Despite so many Scots?"

"It was," she said. "Better than expected, if I am to be honest."

"Was it then?" Agnus frowned as she helped Prudence undress. "Even though you lost your shawl?"

"My shawl?" She touched her shoulders and glanced around, only to realize it was gone. Her mind flashed back to how pleasantly warm she had grown when talking with Jacob at dinner. Had she taken it off, then? She could hardly remember. Agnus did not need to know that, though. "I must have misplaced it along the way."

"Dear me," Agnus said. "I will ask around and see it returned straight away, my lady."

She could tell by Agnus' perplexed expression she found that most unusual because it was. Prudence was meticulous about everything. She would never lose or forget anything.

"Thank you, Miss Agnus." She eyed her maid curiously. "And how has your evening been so far?"

Agnus looked at her oddly as if taken aback that she asked because, truly, she normally would not. Never much cared.

"Fine enough, my lady," she said. "All things considered."

"Right," she murmured. Her thoughts kept wandering back to Jacob. How he fared at that very moment. "Despite them being Scots." She considered Agnus as she sat, and her maid started undoing her hair. "Have you run into much trouble? Or have things been up to your...*our* standards?"

"More up to our standards than expected my lady." Agnus carefully removed the pins. "The staff is well-organized, and things are kept quite clean."

"Good to hear."

"Indeed, my lady."

They said little after that, and Agnus went on her way after Prudence dismissed her. For the first time since arriving, she was tempted to step out onto her balcony. Tempted to put on a warm wrap and breathe in a new sense of freedom that filled her more by the moment. An odd but not unwelcome sensation she rather liked. Relished, if she were to be honest.

The night was chilly, though, and despite being on the quiet side of the castle, what if someone saw her? It would be most inappropriate. So she crawled into bed, lay there for a time, and thought about the evening. Mostly, she thought about the Duke of Argyll, no matter how much she tried to put him from her mind. However foolish the notion, she wondered if she crossed his mind as well. Likely not, as she imagined his thoughts were consumed by his late wife—as they should be.

Which led her back to what he had said in regard to Elizabeth. How he had taken out his anger at her loss through fencing. What anger had he battled before that, though? Should she ask him about it again, or was it a matter best left alone? She would think not, considering he had seemed ready to tell her before they were interrupted.

Either way, she decided it best to let the matter rest as she made her way down to breakfast the next morning. When she found the dining area empty, she decided to pass on eating. No doubt, her sister and Lord MacLauchlin had entertained well into the evening and still rested. As did most, based on how quiet things were.

"Good morning, Lady Barrington." The butler beamed brightly at her when she approached the front door. "Out for a morning stroll?"

Where she had barely taken notice of him upon her arrival, she found his demeanor rather pleasant today, so she met his smile. "I think perhaps I am."

"Very good, my lady." He assisted her with her coat. "While it's quiet after the night's festivities, you might still find a soul or two about. It seems you and the Duke of Argyll are early risers."

"Is the duke outside, then?"

"Aye, my lady." He smiled and opened the door. "He tends to like morning strolls."

Somehow that did not surprise her, given his inherent energy. Or so she assumed him energetic, based on his fitness. It was not just that alone, though. Perhaps the zest for life in his eyes or the excitement she sensed hovering beneath his surface. As if he were just waiting for the formalities to be over so he could move. Do something more exhilarating.

"Thank you..." for the first time in years, she prompted a butler for his name.

The butler's smile only grew wider. His eyes sparkled beneath bushy white brows as he bowed from the waist. "That would be Mr. Finley, my lady, but most in these parts just call me Finley."

"Well, thank you, Finley." She stepped out the door and did yet another thing she had not done in years when she wished a servant a good day.

If possible, Finley's smile grew even wider. "You as well, my lady."

She started down the steps and breathed in the fresh, crisp air. Where she had seen the castle's obvious wealth when she arrived, today she saw the beauty of nature and the glorious grounds. They were well-groomed and quite lovely. More eager than she would admit, she scanned the immediate area for Jacob but saw no sign of him.

*Leave him be regardless*, she chastised herself. It was clear he still faced personal battles. Moreover, he might very well want the time alone. A chance to reflect. Remember.

A strange notion because she had no idea if she had actually felt love for Randolph initially. Knew for certain she did not as time went on. How could she? So she had no idea how it felt to love so deeply and then lose it. The only thing she could possibly compare it to was how she'd felt when she'd realized her husband did not love her. Would never love her. There had been a terrible sense of loss in that, but she suspected it paled in comparison to what Jacob had gone through.

Interested in what lay behind MacLauchlin Castle because she had heard things quite enchanting, she made her way along a winding, tree-covered path that ran alongside it. She could not remember the last time she enjoyed anything like this. Before she married and moved to London, to be sure. Back in her younger years when a trail like this would have ignited her imagination.

A time when she had, in her naiveté, envisioned walking hand in hand with the man she loved at their country estate. Pictured kissing him beneath a verdant canopy of leaves. Making love when they wandered across a sunlit patch of meadow. Giving herself over to how he made her feel.

She inhaled the scent of the pungent, earthy woodland and allowed her imagination to drift even further. To envision strolling, not with her late husband, but with Jacob. She imagined the conversations they might have before he began looking at her in a certain way. Her cheeks warmed at the thought. At how he might gradually steer her closer to him. How it might become obvious by the look in his eyes that he had become less interested in the conversation and more interested in kissing her.

Where moments before she had been chilled, she felt rather overheated now and unbuttoned the first few buttons on her coat. She once again inhaled the crisp air deeply and tried to set aside her wandering thoughts, yet it seemed impossible. How would he go about things? Would he pull her against his strong body? Cup her cheek and close his mouth over hers?

Her thoughts only spiraled from there.

What would his kiss feel like? Would it be like the few her husband had given her over the years? Cold and unfeeling?

Somehow she doubted it.

Jacob had too much passion for that. He would kiss her with the same vigor he had exuded when explaining the portraits. Spoke of Scottish history. Of the various dishes being served. She would have his undivided attention. He would see only her. Only ever her as he swept her up into his arms and carried her to a private sunlit patch of meadow laden with wildflowers.

To their own little oasis nuzzled in the trees.

Or so her ridiculous and foolhardy mind thought of a man she barely knew. That she had loathed not a day ago. With good reason, too, when she spied him around the backside of the castle. He was not sitting alone, deep in thought, pining over his late wife but doing quite the opposite. Rather, he strolled in the hedge gardens below with a beautiful woman on his arm. Smiled at her. Laughed with her.

Clearly adored spending time with her.

Her stomach sank at how foolish she had been. What had she been thinking letting her guard down for even a moment? For imagining they might have been forming some sort of connection the night before? That she might ever enjoy a kiss of all things with him. Shame on her. She knew better.

*Preposterous.*

Before he caught sight of her, she headed back the way she had come. Enough was enough. The Lord of Argyll was everything she had thought him. A scoundrel, to be sure. One she would make sure to avoid at all costs until she left first thing tomorrow morning.

# Chapter Six

"BLOODY HELL," JACOB cursed under his breath when he saw Prudence appear beside the castle at the top of the path leading down to the hedge gardens. Utterly lovely with an almost whimsical dewy sparkle in her blue eyes, she had seemed lost in thought, daydreaming perhaps, before she focused on him and his former cousin-by-marriage, Emma. Before he had a chance to wave her over, she spun on her heel and vanished.

"Oh, dear." Emma glanced at him with concern. "She did not appear pleased to see us together, did she? Most certainly took things all wrong?"

"Aye." He scowled and shook his head. "As you well know, Lady Barrington has a way of doing that."

"So I have heard." They continued strolling as they tended to do at this hour if they were visiting MacLauchlin Castle at the same time. "Though I must admit she does not appear the grotesque monster I have long envisioned her."

"No," he said softly, contemplating Prudence, "she is any-thing but."

He had not only enjoyed showing her around the castle yes-terday but very much liked dining with her. And of course, looking at her had been a pleasure. She had a way of rubbing her lips together when thinking about something that left them rosy, plush, and distractingly tempting. A new light had shimmered in her eyes, and her expressions had become less stiff and more varied. It almost seemed like she'd blossomed in front of his eyes in one day's time. As if she were just waiting for the right person to come along. The perfect opportunity.

Not only did she ask plenty of questions, but she'd even smiled. Not laughed. He had not pulled that much from her yet but sensed it was possible and spent the better part of the night wondering what that would look like. Regrettably, pleasure and anticipation turned to guilt when he heard Elizabeth's pianoforte being played. A poignant reminder of the time they had spent together in this very castle.

"I noticed you and Lady Barrington spent quite a bit of time together yesterday." Emma gave him a knowing look. "I will admit, I found it interesting you did not introduce us."

"You were never around to introduce." However much he had hoped to avoid this, he knew it would be brought up eventually. Knew Emma would see right through him if he offered anything but the truth. "And if you were, I still might have hesitated."

Emma might be his age, but she had always been wiser and more perceptive than most. Seen clearly in the way she stopped him. "Dear cousin, know this and know it well. You might not have seen me, but I saw you. More than that, I saw you and her together." She looked at him in the affectionate, forgiving way few could. "So I know despite your need to save her from herself, you might finally be ready to save yourself as well."

As much as her words might seem twisted to most, he understood her meaning.

"I enjoyed her company," he admitted, hoping she did not hear the emotion in his voice. "Far more than expected when it should have been the last thing on my mind the moment Elizabeth's pianoforte arrived."

"Whatever for?" Emma tilted her head. "I know you are on a mission to help lasses who were like you before Elizabeth came into your life, and you have. Perhaps now, you can let all that go and move on?"

"I have moved on," he said, even though their very conversation proved otherwise. "There is just something…different about her. Something that very much draws me to her."

Emma glanced from where Prudence had vanished back to him. "I hazard to say she might feel the same about you based on the way she fled so quickly when she saw me on your arm."

"You say that as though the others I pursued after Elizabeth would not have done the same."

"Oh, I am sure they would have." Emma shook her head. "Only they would not have had the same look in their eyes." She offered the sort of smile that put him at ease. "More to the point had they, I doubt it would have upset you so. You would have responded with the utmost confidence that you would smooth everything over in good time."

He narrowed his eyes and offered a crooked grin. Tried to keep things lighthearted when in truth, she was right, and it unsettled him. "Did you gather all that from a brief glance across the way, then?"

"I gathered everything I needed to know when I saw you and Lady Barrington together yesterday." She winked. "And lest it weigh on your mind what I thought of her slanderous tongue years ago, I beg you, do not. I might have detested her actions, but like you, I am well aware of her late husband's frivolous, awful ways, so I understand how she might have become wounded. Impulsive. Hateful, even." She rested her hand on his arm in comfort. Understanding. "That said, I would never fault you for loving her if that is what you two find, Jacob. And I do believe Elizabeth would feel the same."

Very few opinions meant more, and he appreciated it. Emma and Elizabeth had been close. So close, Emma had become more like a sister-by-marriage over the years.

"While I am nowhere near loving Lady Barrington, I appreciate your support." He steered her toward the castle. "Now let us return before Lord Campbell wakes and comes looking for you."

"Come now." She chuckled, not afraid to be blunt. "My husband and I were long awake before I took my morning stroll."

No doubt they were, as they shared a love similar to what he and Elizabeth had experienced. The same sort Blake had with Maude. A coming together where there could be no question desire existed despite how discreet the couple thought themselves. A ravenous love that would undoubtedly last into their old age.

Could that sort of love exist for him again? Would he ever find anything like what he shared with Elizabeth? It seemed impossible. Yet he could admit for the first time in longer than he could remember, despite mourning for her when the piano had started playing the night before, his mind had time and time again wandered back to Prudence. The light in her eyes when she asked this question or that. Her avid and genuine curiosity when he answered.

In some ways, she reminded him of Elizabeth, but in most ways, they were nothing alike. Where his late wife had always meant well, she had no real interest in history or weapons. Nor had she ever spoken bluntly to him if she found his explanations not quite right. Not like Prudence did. If Lady Barrington found something unbelievable or too far-fetched, she would need to understand it. In all honesty, he suspected she might enjoy a healthy debate as much as he.

Then there were the other thoughts he had done his best to push aside as he walked the grounds last night to escape the piano music and memories. Thoughts that had everything to do with Prudence. How the color of her eyes seemed to shift with her mood. How her skin flushed when her excitement heightened about certain subjects.

He had never seen a woman grow so passionate about what most lasses might consider boring. Or for that matter, be interested in subjects where she learned something new. Especially when it was about a country she seemed to dislike hours before. Did he think her mad because of it? Not at all.

Which might make him as mad as her.

Or, as Emma had implied, there was something more to all this.

More to the feelings awakening inside him when it came to Lady Barrington. Something he very much hoped to get to the bottom of in good time. That is, if she would still give him time after seeing him and Emma together.

It seemed he had truly miffed her because every opportunity throughout the day he thought he might be able to speak with her, she turned away and drifted in the opposite direction. To the point, he knew seeing him with Emma had bothered her.

While frustrated, he could admit to being elated if for no other reason than what made her so upset in the first place. She had not liked seeing him alone with another woman. More specifically, she had been jealous. He was certain of it. And while he disliked her feeling such, he *did* like what it might mean for them going forward. It seemed he might just be able to woo the uppity Lady Barrington after all.

Truth be told, he could think of nothing else he would rather do.

So, despite her avoiding him at every turn, he made sure arrangements were made for traveling to the festival and took advantage of a brief respite when men were not fawning over her to approach before she darted away.

"Lady Barrington." He bowed his head, then issued his most winning smile. "I feared I might never catch up with you today."

"Your Grace." She curtsied, her gaze not shy but rather direct, if not cold. "So lovely to see you again."

"You as well." He looked at those leaving the great hall. "Everyone is traveling into town for the St. Cecilia's festivities. I was wondering if you might join me?"

"I thank you for your kind offer, Your Grace," she replied almost haughtily despite him ranking above her, "but I have already accepted my sister's invitation to join her."

"She has," Blake said, joining them right on time. He played along because what else were good friends for? Blake flinched and cast Prudence an apologetic look. "But I am afraid unexpected guests have since arrived who really must travel with Lady MacLauchlin and me." He glanced from Jacob to Prudence, hopeful. "Would it be too much of a bother riding with the Duke of Argyll instead?"

"You would be most welcome." Keeping his voice loud enough for all to hear, Jacob gave her no room to escape. "Please do ride with me, Lady Barrington? I insist."

"That would be lovely, Your Grace." Prudence's eyes narrowed ever so slightly, but what else could she do but nod? As it were, a duke had requested her company.

"Very good." He smiled, put his hand to the small of her back, and steered her toward his carriage before she came up with some sort of clever way out of it. "I look forward to today's festivities, my lady."

She did not respond, but then he had not expected her to. Rather, she remained the closed-off shell she was days ago as Finley helped her with her jacket, and they made their way down to his carriage. There was no missing her tight expression as they sat opposite Emma and her husband. He need not read her mind to know precisely what she thought. So he made things plain straight away and introduced them.

"Lady Barrington, meet Lord and Lady Campbell," he said. "Emma is my late wife's cousin and a dear friend, as is her husband."

Where he thought that would make all the difference, Prudence's expression only grew tighter after she greeted them and turned her attention to the landscape. When he glanced at Emma, she merely offered a slight shrug. One that told him he might have underestimated just how deeply Prudence's husband had wounded her. That even relatives by marriage, however preposterous the notion, were not off the table of possible offenders.

Everyone made polite conversation as they traveled, but it

felt uncomfortable. Formal. Too formal, considering what he had started to see blossom within Prudence the day before. So rather than ignore the strain between them, he broached it after they arrived, bid Emma and her husband an enjoyable time, and went their own way.

"Might we take a moment to talk, Lady Barrington?" He offered her his elbow. "Because I sense something has changed since we parted ways last night."

"Whatever do you mean?" Her voice was as tight as her pursed lips. She looked anywhere but at him, as she slipped her arm into his out of obligation. "Rest assured, all is well, Your Grace."

"Call me Jacob."

She straightened as if slapped. "Certainly *not*, Your Grace."

He smiled at her like he had the night before. Like he had wanted to since the moment she was gracious enough to give him time alone to mourn his late wife. "Why when I asked it of you? Because—"

"No." She shook her head sharply but did not pull away as too many people smiled and curtsied their way. "That is *most* inappropriate, and I will not."

"Then let us take a moment so I can show you something." He turned off the beaten path until they ended up in a rather secluded spot between two buildings. "What do you see?"

She tensed, glanced from building to building, and frowned. "What do you mean?"

"I mean, what do you see when you look at these buildings?"

Her frown deepened. "I see nothing but old abodes."

"Really?" He perked a brow. "Because they are much more than that."

Where he thought her interest might be piqued by their whereabouts, it seemed she had gotten the wrong idea. So said the way she stopped short, gazed around to make sure no one was looking, then narrowed her eyes at him. "Whatever you are about, I *will* not be part of it." She shook her head. "I do not participate in secret rendezvous with men out of wedlock."

"Duly noted, my lady, so rest assured that is not why I brought you here." Where some might be offended, he was no such thing. "Rather, I wanted to show you what Lady Campbell and I were talking about this morning when you came upon us. The business venture, or project if you will, that I have undertaken with the Campbells and MacLauchlins to resurrect old landmarks throughout Scotland. A means to keep our country's history alive."

"That is a noble cause." Though it remained clear she thought he and Emma discussed far more. Flirted, to be precise. "Why are you telling me this?"

"Because you showed an interest in history, for starters." Not about to skirt the issue, he gave her a pointed look. "And because I would rather you not think poorly of Lady Campbell when I can assure you, she would never be unfaithful to her husband. Nor would I ever ask it of her if I had designs on her, to begin with."

He could tell by Prudence's rosy cheeks that the topic made her uncomfortable. Nevertheless, her assumption that he had brought her here for a secret rendezvous had, by its very nature, opened up a more forthright dialogue between them. One, despite her embarrassment, she took advantage of in a roundabout way.

"Rest assured, I could care less about the nature of your relationship with Lady Campbell," she bit out. "But I can tell you without question had Lord Campbell come upon you two, he might very well have seen something quite untoward in the intimate way you conversed."

"Or," he countered, "he might have seen dear friends enjoying one another's company rather than flirtation." He reminded her how easily her perception could be skewed. "For there is such a thing as merely enjoying the company of a friend, even if they are of the opposite sex. Such a thing as enjoying good conversation and smiling at a woman whilst not wanting anything more." He flinched. "Especially when they are kin."

He could tell by her dubious look she had trouble believing such. She remained unconvinced he was not like her late husband, and no different than she had thought him years ago.

"Be that as it may, Your Grace—" she straightened and tipped her chin in indignation. chin—"I have come to the conclusion that, while grateful for your company since arriving at MacLauchlin Castle, it might be misinterpreted if we spend too much time together. Therefore, I shall return to Mayfair first thing in the morning." She curtsied. "Enjoy the rest of the celebrations."

Stubborn woman. He wanted to tell her he was not a womanizer. Make her understand just how taken he had become with her in such a short time. How to handle this now? How to find his way back to where they had left off the night before? It seemed an impossible feat. Or so he assumed until he realized just how much others wanted them to find their way back there too.

# Chapter Seven

WHILE PRUDENCE COULD admit a part of her was relieved when she found out Lady Campbell was the Duke of Argyll's cousin by marriage, another part feared it would not matter. That, however unfortunate the notion, not being an actual blood relation, could very well make all the difference.

"Ah, there you are, dear sister." Maude joined her and smiled. "Where did you get off to?" She glanced from where the duke had reappeared to Prudence and offered a knowing grin. "I see."

"You see nothing." However ill-timed, this little interlude with her sister gave her the perfect opportunity to see how truthful Jacob had been. "The duke was merely showing me the buildings he is investing in with you and the Campbells."

"Indeed we are." Maude slipped her arm into Prudence's as they made their way down a quaint street full of vendors. "Such a worthy undertaking, is it not?" Her eyes sparkled with excitement. "It was the duke's idea in the first place. A means to give back to his country. So we were eager to join him when he asked us."

Prudence tried to respond but could not get a word in edgewise.

"Personally, I think in some small way, it was a means to help him heal from his late wife's loss." Maude sighed sadly. "While he could not stop her from wasting away when illness took her, he *could* bring back Scotland piece by piece. While I do not know if the late duchess enjoyed history, she did love her country fiercely." She glanced in the Campbells' direction. "I think our joint project helped Lady Campbell just as much."

"She was close with the late duchess, then?"

"Very," Maude said. "I am told they were like sisters. That the Rothesays, as they were known at the time, and the Campbells were very close."

"Perhaps too close?" Prudence ventured.

Maude looked at her in confusion before her eyebrows shot up and understanding dawned. "Oh, good Lord, no, never like that." She made the sign of the cross over her chest. "That would be incest not only because they are kin by marriage but because Jacob and Emma very much look at each other like siblings." Her gaze narrowed between Jacob, who had just joined the Campbells, and Prudence. "Surely, you did not think otherwise?"

"Of course not," she said a little too quickly, fearing perhaps she had once again seen something that was not there.

"I would hope not." Yet Maude's gaze grew all-too-knowing again as it flickered between Jacob and Prudence. "Though it *would* explain why you avoided him today when I thought you two had hit it off quite nicely yesterday."

"I was not avoiding him." Though she very much had been. "There were simply others whose company I wished to enjoy. It would be unseemly had I ignored them and spent all my time with the duke."

"No doubt." A little smirk hovered on Maude's mouth. "Who would want to spend all their time with a duke? Very unseemly, to be sure."

Rather than respond, Prudence focused on their surroundings and felt more foolish by the moment. Especially given what she had said when Jacob showed her the buildings he intended to resurrect. Buildings he very likely intended to tell her more about, considering how much she enjoyed history.

She could only imagine what he thought when she implied he

meant to take her into one of them and have his way with her. If that was not mortifying enough, her blasphemous thoughts kept wandering back to how it might have felt.

How he might touch her.

Naturally, the idea he would want to enjoy her like that after what she had done years ago seemed farfetched. Not only that, but he was a handsome eligible duke in his prime who could have his pick of the litter. To her mind, that most certainly would not include spinsters such as herself. Even so, her skin flushed, and her traitorous thoughts kept wandering.

Suffice it to say she did her best to avoid him, only this time out of embarrassment rather than frustration. She was certain she should apologize but had no idea where to begin. Would she be apologizing for her behavior of years ago or of this very afternoon? Because the more she had thought about it lying in bed last night, the more certain she grew that she might have seen something years ago that was not there. Just as she had seen something that was not there this morning.

As it happened, the celebrations in the quaint Scottish town were lovely. A variety of musicians had come to play and commission work. Some played fiddles. Others, bagpipes. When she stopped and listened, she could admit their sound was soulful. Haunting, almost. As if they told a story only these Scots were privy to.

One she imagined Jacob would tell her if he stood with her now.

In fact, he probably would have educated her a great deal about this town, its inhabitants, and, as he had already tried, the older buildings. She might have spent a pleasant afternoon learning many things from an entertaining companion rather than be alone because she assumed every man she met had rotten intentions.

"And now that you are in the right frame of mind," Grace would likely say. "Why not set aside your pride and tell him you are sorry? Why not start anew and enjoy the rest of your day with an amiable companion?"

If only it were that easy. Every time she glanced his way, Jacob was talking to one villager or another. By all appearances, he appeared to enjoy those who were less fortunate than him. By the way he laughed and chatted with them, he thought himself no better. An impression that aligned with how he had spoken about his countrymen the day before.

Unfortunately, the few times he was alone, she could not muster the courage to approach him, and before she knew it, it was time to head back to the castle. This go around, she rode with her sister and Lord MacLauchlin.

"I do hope you enjoyed your day, sister." Maude smiled at her husband. "These Scots truly do know how to enjoy themselves."

"Aye, lass." He looked at Maude with unmistakable affection. "It is very much in our blood."

"No doubt it is." Maude turned her smile Prudence's way. "And there is still so much more fun to be had. There will be dancing this evening and two more days of the festival, including church on Sunday, of course." Her smile faded beneath a dainty pout. "Which I do so hope you will attend with us rather than fleeing back to Mayfair?"

Had the duke told her as much? He must have because only he and Agnus knew of her plans to leave tomorrow. Her heart gave a strange little flutter. Why had he shared such? Could it be because he did not want her to leave and hoped her sister might stop her? Or because he wanted to make sure Maude saw Prudence off, so he never had to see her again?

"As you might expect, I was quite sorry to hear you might be leaving so soon," Maude said, answering her question as if she knew where Prudence's thoughts had gone. "As was the duke when he shared the unfortunate news with Blake and me. He was quite crestfallen if I did not know better." Her sister tilted her head at her husband in question. "Would you not agree, my love?"

Where she had been put off by Maude's familiarity with Lord MacLauchlin before, she could care less now. Rather, she waited with bated breath. Or at least that was how it felt when her breathing grew uncomfortably shallow.

"I would very much agree." Blake smiled kindly at Prudence. "It seems you have a new friend in the Duke of Argyll. He was hoping to enjoy more of your company before you departed."

Was he really? After her behavior earlier? "Though I really should press on and not overstay my welcome, we shall see."

"A welcome that was supposed to be indefinite," Maude reminded her. "Until you decide where you will go next, which, the last I understood it, was not Mayfair ever again if you could help it."

"I never said such." Had she?

"Well, you should have."

"I *do* live there, sister."

"You did," Maude granted. "But I would highly recommend never doing so again."

She could not agree more, but she had nowhere else to go. Thankfully, they arrived at the castle shortly thereafter, so Maude could not go on about it. Instead, Prudence was left to her own devices, which meant visiting with several gentlemen she could not slip by before returning to her chamber to get a good night's rest.

Which, as Maude would have it, would be after a bath, compliments of maids who were every bit as efficient as Agnus claimed. They even went so far as to provide a flower-scented wash ball and a warm towel.

"How did your day go, my lady?" Agnus assisted her into the bath. "Despite your desire to leave this morning."

"Better than I might have imagined." The water felt pleasantly warm against her cool skin. "The festival was interesting. Quite lively." She glanced at her maid. "You should try to find your way there tomorrow. I believe you might enjoy it."

"Goodness, no." Although Agnus seemed properly taken

aback by that, Prudence swore she saw a glimmer of interest in her maid's typically hard gaze. "Will we not be leaving then, my lady?"

"I remain undecided." Though she was not. "It seems my sister very much wants me to attend church with her on Sunday, and I cannot see how I can deny her."

"That *is* a hard thing to deny."

"Even so." Prudence gestured at the day's clothing. "Might you see those cleaned below stairs and prepared for travel?"

"Of course, my lady."

When Prudence perked an eyebrow at her maid, she seemed surprised.

"You mean now while you bathe?" Agnus said.

"I do," she said. "If you would?"

"If that is what you wish, my lady." Agnus gathered up her clothing. "I will return straight away."

She thanked her and released a sigh of relief when she left. Relief that she could take a moment alone with her thoughts which, as seemed to be the ongoing case, were solely focused on Jacob. Did he truly want her to stay? If so, was it, as Maude and Blake implied, because he enjoyed her company in a purely platonic fashion? Or could it be more? She had absolutely no clue.

Interestingly, she found either option to be acceptable but could admit she hoped it might be friendship at first. That he might simply enjoy talking with her. Spending time together. While that could be in part her own insecurity that a man would ever be interested in more, the idea of companionship with him was most appealing. Perhaps because it would be just that. As it were, the Duke of Argyll was not in need of money, or the esteem being married to a former earl's wife could bring.

She rested her head back against the tub and closed her eyes. Tried to envision what a friendship with Jacob might look like. Yet her thoughts inevitably drifted to how it would feel if it were more. What it might be like if, years from now, they visited this castle, and he opened her chamber door instead of Agnus. If he crouched beside her bath and slid his hand into the water. If he trailed it from her chest, down between her breasts, over her stomach, then lower. Slow. So slowly, breathing became impossible.

Would he touch her where she began to throb, or would he tease her more? Trail his fingers further down her quivering thigh, or assuage the growing ache inside her?

Her eyes flew open when a light rap came at the door. Startled, she gripped the side of the tub when she realized her own hand had traveled in the wake of her fantasy. For a split second, she imagined Jacob might actually be standing on the other side of her door but set aside the silly notion when Agnus entered.

"Will you be attending dinner below stairs?" Her maid wrapped a towel around her when she stepped out of the bath. "Or dining in this evening?"

While she had been set to dine alone, the sound of music drifting up when Agnus opened the door had been enticing. The thought of seeing Jacob, even across the room, was even more alluring.

"I think I will dine below stairs, after all."

"Very good." Her maid opened the armoire only to stop short.

"What is it, Miss Agnus?"

"Something most unexpected, my lady." Agnus frowned and stepped aside so she could see. "Everything but one of the dresses Lady MacLauchlin provided is missing." She pulled out a small scroll tucked into its cleavage and handed it to Prudence. "It appears this might be for you."

"Without doubt." She unrolled it, read the brief note from her sister, and outright scowled at her sister's nerve. "It seems Lady MacLauchlin was kind enough to have all my gowns properly seen to for my travels tomorrow."

"Is that not strange, my lady?"

"Very, but this is Maude we are talking about." She highly doubted her clothing was anywhere but tucked away in this castle somewhere, forcing Prudence to dress differently for the first time in ages.

Well, two could play at that game.

"My sister thinks to force my hand." She narrowed her eyes. "What she forgets is I have the option not to attend at all. Fetch my night rail."

"Of course, my lady." Agnus opened a bureau drawer only to pause again. "If I could, that is."

"Surely *not*." She joined her maid and stared down into the nearly empty drawer. There was nothing left but undergarments appropriate for the gown. "Oh, blast her!"

When Agnus looked at her in astonishment, Prudence apologized for her language, but good Lord, she meant it.

"I will go below stairs straight away and seek a night rail, my lady." Agnus's brow furrowed. "For shame, I will *demand* it."

"Demand though you might, I suspect you will not find a suitable night rail in all of MacLauchlin Castle," she said dryly. "Likely not the whole of Scotland if my sister has her way."

She sighed and considered the short-sleeved gown. Was it appropriate to wear such a garment? What might people think? Many women embraced color the moment they were out of mourning. Far brighter colors than the muted gold of the gown. Styles that were even more daring.

*"And with good reason," Grace would say, "as they are out of mourning. Moreover, might you not be going against decorum if you continued dressing so darkly? Going against what would be expected of you at this point? Which would, in its own way, be in defiance of good sense, yes?"*

"You make a good point," she murmured.

"What is that?" Agnus said.

Surprised she had spoken aloud, she blinked, waved it off, and came to a swift decision. "I will wear it." She gathered her courage and nodded at her maid. "I will wear the gown provided and attend the festivities below."

Agnus' eyebrows edged up slowly. "Are you quite sure, my

lady?"

"I am."

Or better put, whether she was or not, she intended to be. Would she have a word or two to say to her sister? Undoubtedly. But she could admit being forced into this was not the worst thing. Or so she thought until she slid into the dress and realized it was every bit as revealing as she had feared. Her cleavage appeared far too full. Plumper than she realized her breasts could be.

"This is highly indecent." She sat, pulled on matching elbow-length silk gloves, and let Agnus fashion her hair into a high bun with loose curls framing her face. "I will be most looked down upon wearing something like this at my age."

When Agnus remained unnaturally silent, she caught her gaze in the mirror. "What is it?" Prudence prompted her again when she hesitated. "Just tell me. Should I undress at once? Retire until you can find me a night rail in this God-forsaken castle?"

"Quite the opposite," Agnus finally said, draping a delicate pearl necklace around her neck. "I think you look beautiful, my lady. Elegant, to be sure. And I dare say, I have seen far older ladies in more revealing dresses than this." Her voice dropped an octave, and she became bolder still. "Ladies who should have perhaps refrained from such gowns where you should do no such thing."

What had come over her sturdy, detached maid? Was she ill? She asked as much, too, before she could stop herself.

"I am not ill, my lady." After Agnus clipped pearl drop ear-rings on Prudence's earlobes, she urged her to face the full-length mirror and wrapped a sheer shawl around her shoulders that accented the dress beautifully. "I am merely offering you the truth. Something you tend to prefer if I am not mistaken?"

"Quite right," she said softly when she saw her reflection. She was so transformed it almost seemed, yet again, that a stranger stared back. While no longer a blossoming young woman dressed for her coming out ball, some might say her equally lovely in a different way. As Agnus had implied, a more elegant version. There was a becoming rosiness to her cheeks she did not recall being there upon her arrival. A sparkle to her eyes that had been missing.

The dress almost seemed hand-tailored for her. Most definitely, her sister's doing. It flattered her in all the right areas, and while the neckline was a bit lower than she would have liked, it did not seem as tasteless as she originally thought. Rather, it made her feel sumptuous when combined with the shawl. Confident in a way that made little sense.

Moreover, it seemed to remove several more bars from her rhetorical cage.

No doubt, it was one more rung toward the freedom she had started to feel yesterday. One more step away from Mayfair and her late husband. Which led her to wonder, for the first time in longer than she could remember, how men might see her.

More specifically, how the Duke of Argyll might see her.

Would he find her alluring? Did she truly want him to, or was it best to continue hoping for mere friendship? To seek out what she needed above all right now? Companionship. A connection of the mind because she had begun to realize that's what she needed more and more. Understood it after talking with Jacob. She had never done something like that with a man before and quite liked it. Liked who she was when conversing about subjects she enjoyed.

Even though she felt a moment of reluctance when she eventually headed downstairs, she squared her shoulders and pressed on. She was glad she did, too. Glad she faced this alone rather than with her sister or even a man. Liked the feeling of standing on her own two feet out from under the low-hanging cloud of her late husband. Free of his watchful, disappointed eyes.

Free to enjoy the appreciative gazes of men admiring her as she headed downstairs and crossed the great hall. They were not calculative looks hungry for wealth this time, but genuine admiration. Desire, if she were not mistaken. Looks she could not remember receiving even in her blooming youth. Why would she when her late husband had swooped in so quickly? When she only had eyes for him at the beginning?

Just as, at this very moment, she could only see Jacob when he appeared in front of her. Better still, as her fanciful mind would have it, he could only see her.

# Chapter Eight

WHILE JACOB ENJOYED the day's festivities, he would be lying if he said he had not wished to enjoy them with Prudence by his side. He'd wanted to show her every little thing. Explain his culture, from the design of the cottages to his people's traditions at festivals.

Instead, he watched her from afar and hoped she enjoyed herself. While she had seemed interested in her surroundings, he could not help but notice she appeared especially taken with the bagpipes. They might be played plenty in England nowadays, but he got the distinct impression she heard them differently in a small Scottish village. Felt them in a way few of her ilk did. He had desired more than ever to be by her side, discussing her thoughts. How everything affected her.

Yet, as the day wore on, she'd kept her distance. Or should he say he kept his distance because he had no choice. At this point, it was up to her to come to him if she desired his company. And he had stuck to that no matter how difficult.

At least until he spied her coming down the stairs that evening.

Until he saw her out of anything resembling mourning clothes and in a dress that seemed handspun by the angels. Saints above, she was a vision, and every hot-blooded man in the room knew it as their gazes turned her way. Her chestnut locks shimmered in the candlelight and her flawless skin appeared luminescent. Moreover, the way her dress hugged her lush curves fueled one's imagination indeed. To the best of his knowledge, she had decided to remain in her room for the evening. So why the sudden change of heart? Better yet, why such a monumental leap in appearance?

Whatever her reasons, he very much approved. So much so that he drifted her way despite his determination to let her come to him. Drifted until he stood in front of her. If that were not enough, wanting her nowhere but with him, his mouth and actions seemed to have a mind of their own.

"My lady." He held out his elbow, giving her no choice but to accept his invitation. "Might you join me for dinner?"

He was unsure if her eyes flashed with defiance or relief when she curtsied and slid her arm into his, but he was determined to find out. Discover as much as he possibly could about her before she tried to dart away again. Did she still intend to leave tomorrow? Or might they be able to spend more time together after the night was over?

Prudence said little as chestnut soup was served, followed by mackerel with fennel and mint. He had not expected her to say much, though. Not right away. Not with so many people around in such a lively, talkative mood. She did cast him cordial glances every so often, though. Mayhap, as his hopeful mind would have it, because she was as aware of him as he was of her.

Eventually, diners drifted off in the direction of the music, eager to dance, and he and Prudence were alone. He knew by the way she traced her finger back and forth over the bottom of her glass that her nerves ran high. She struggled to say something to him but seemed unable to find the right words.

"Might we join the others and—"

"Yes," she said, cutting him off. Her cheeks grew rosy. "What I mean to say is you have my apologies, Your Grace." Her breathing might be irregular, but she still managed to look him in the eyes. "Not just for interrupting you but for my behavior earlier today. For—" she cleared her throat and folded her ever-so-slightly shaky hands on her lap—"for thinking you would be so uncouth." Her delicate cheekbones grew even rosier. "For thinking—"

"All is well, Lady Barrington."

She went perfectly still when he rested his hand over hers and offered a warm, forgiving smile.

"I do not fault your assumptions," he went on. "Nor do I wish you to feel guilt over what lies in our past, be it recent or distant."

Her gaze flickered from his hand to his face, and her pupils flared. "That is generous of you, Your Grace."

"Jacob."

"No," she said softly, her blush only deepening.

"Perhaps someday?"

"Unlikely."

He searched her eyes. "Are you sure?"

Her gaze lingered on his face. "Not at all."

"Good," he said just as softly, aroused at the implication. While he wanted to say one thing, he sensed it best to voice another for now. "Because my dearest friends call me by my given name, and I do hope you will be such someday, as I find you most interesting."

"As do I, you," she replied quickly enough to satisfy him. Satisfy her, too, based on the way tension eased from her shoulders.

He arched a brow. "Then might we begin anew once again, my lady?"

She met his small smile. "I would like that."

"Excellent." While he wanted to keep touching her soft hands, intimacy was not what she needed right now. So he stood and bowed at the waist. "It is very nice to make your acquaintance, Lady Barrington." He held out his elbow. "Might I show you around the parts of MacLauchlin Castle you might not have seen on previous tours?"

"It is very nice to make your acquaintance as well, Your

Grace." She stood and curtsied before slipping her arm into his. "Thank you ever so much for your offer. While a pleasant, informative gentleman gave me a tour yesterday, I must admit I long to see more. Therefore, your offer sounds delightful." A smile hovered on her delectable mouth. "Are you up to the challenge, though, I wonder?

"Very much so." While she was most certainly playing along, he could not help but wonder. Was the prim and proper Lady Barrington actually *flirting*? "I think you might find my knowledge of this castle quite sound."

"I would hope so, given your confidence."

He chuckled. "As would I."

Fortunately, their playful banter continued, and with drinks in hand, they resumed their tour of the castle. Where he most certainly enjoyed yesterday with her, tonight was all that much better. Not because she looked so stunning, as he found her just as alluring the eve before, but because there was a new ease between them. A comfortable comradery he quite liked.

They started with a tour of the second floor, beginning with an introduction to the numerous ancestors peering down from portraits overlooking the staircase. "From the three MacLauchlin brothers who resurrected this castle post-war centuries ago to all their descendants, many interesting characters have called this castle home." He gestured at one lass in particular. "Most especially, Lady Annabel."

"Do tell." Prudence gazed up at the painting. Her lovely eyes flashed with excitement. "Because she does look quite mysterious, does she not?"

"Some think so." He led her to the top of the stairs and gestured at the hallway to their right. "Especially those who believed Harrowing Hall was once haunted."

He liked how her eyes continued sparkling with anticipation. How they had a way of making him feel what she felt.

"Oh, but for tall tales." Prudence looked skyward. "As Maude did gush about it a time or two in her letters." She rounded her eyes at him. "Surely, you did not believe all that silliness."

"Not really." They strolled that way. "But I did like how it brought Lord and Lady MacLauchlin even closer together."

"A ghost that was not real?"

"At least not to us." He shrugged. "But it was to them, and that was what mattered most."

"I suppose you must be right." She considered it. "I imagine common ground is helpful."

"As would I."

"Did you share such with your late wife?" Prudence's hand fluttered to her chest. Her brow furrowed. "Apologies, Your Grace. It is not like me to speak so out of turn. I beg of you to dismiss the question."

"I will do no such thing," he said, grateful she had been comfortable enough to ask. It opened the door to asking about her marriage down the line and helping her heal from it. "I do not mind speaking of my late wife." He gave her a pointed look. "Especially to friends. That said, I did share common ground with Elizabeth, and it was beneficial to my marriage. Very much so."

In truth, he shared more common ground with Prudence, but it was far too soon to say so.

"That is lovely to hear," she said, clearly dubious. "Though I am afraid I will have to take your word for such being beneficial to a marriage."

Which told him everything he suspected of her late husband. The two shared nothing in common. But then, he could not see Barrington being the sort to care much about having friendships with women. Not when he had made it clear to anyone willing to listen that the fairer sex was only good for breeding and pleasuring him.

While tempted to continue the conversation, it was better left for another time because there *would* be another time. He grew certain of it as he showed her around, and they became more comfortable with one another. In fact, he could not remember the last time he had enjoyed someone's company as much.

"I will have to take you onto the battlements before your stay here is over," he said after he showed her around for what felt like minutes but was actually hours. Time passed differently with her. Far too quickly. How could it not when she was so interesting? Inquisitive? Brilliant? "I think you might enjoy the architecture up close, not to mention the astounding view."

"I would like that."

"Then you will stay on through the St. Cecilia celebrations?" He paused before they got to the top of the stairs going back down to the great hall and looked at her. "Please say you will remain a few more days, my lady." *For me. Us. Where I believe this might go.* "It would be a shame to deny yourself the entire tour of MacLauchlin Castle."

"It would," she granted, considering it.

He knew better than demand she did anything or even request it of her too strongly. Rather, it was best she felt staying was on her terms, and he had nothing to do with her decision.

"Then do consider it." Certain she knew what was happening between their servants, he grinned. While it was dicey to think it might sway her to rethink things, it was worth a go. "Otherwise, you might deny the MacLauchlin staff from enjoying more banter between your lady's maid and my valet."

Her eyes widened. "Surely *not.*"

"Ah, but a castle does know how to keep its secrets from we high and mighty, does it not?" He steered her a tad closer as they started down the stairs and spoke out of the corner of his mouth in a co-conspirator fashion. "Whilst your maid cannot be blamed, as my valet, Mr. Donal, has a reputation of running a tight ship when we visit others, it seems she runs an even tighter ship. To the point their paths have crossed for whatever reason, and neither much liked each other." He offered a crooked grin. "More specifically, she thought him a loathsome beast."

Prudence narrowed her eyes and replied just as discreetly. "Well, is he?"

"I would say not." He laughed. "But he does have a way of

distrusting most and making that known."

"Why would he ever distrust Miss Agnus?"

"I do not know other than, upon investigation, Lord MacLauchlin would only say it was unfounded." He winked. "So fear not, fair lady, your maid's honor is intact."

"Good news, indeed," she said. "Though I cannot help but wonder…." The corner of her mouth curled up as well. "Was this dramatic tidbit of gossip the best way to go about convincing me to stay?"

"Likely not." He chuckled again. "But one does have to wonder where it may go as I cannot envision such passion from my rather stalwart valet. Most irregular." While tempted to be obtuse lest she flee again, he stopped and gave her at least part of the truth. "I want you to stay because I enjoy your company, Lady Barrington. Because I fear I would grow fatally bored minutes after your departure."

Where he thought, by the tentative look on her face, she would stick to her criteria, she did anything but. Rather, she surprised him. Shocked him, actually.

"I dare say, would it take whole minutes for you to grow bored after my departure?" A shy smile turned her face that much lovelier. "And here I thought it would take but seconds."

"You might very well be right." And may she keep up with her flirtatious banter. He met her smile. "So you will stay on a wee bit? Allow me to give you the full tour? Perhaps even enjoy the ongoing festival in town with me?"

"I will stay on," she said. "But only under one condition."

"Anything."

"Should you not ask what before agreeing?"

"That is not a habit I make when committing to friends," he said, never more serious. "So, name your condition."

He thought for sure it would have to do with keeping things purely platonic, but it seemed she shared the same sense of adventure as him.

"That we will get to the bottom of the strife betwixt Miss

Agnus and Mr. Donal." Prudence offered the sort of grin he could get used to. "And perhaps put an end to it." She once again surprised him when she winked. "Or help it along if there is something more to it?"

"Surely, you do not think…."

"Well, why not?" She shrugged. "Can love not happen in the most unlikely places?"

She truly *was* flirting, was she not? He could only pray. Because last he knew, or very much assumed, Lady Barrington was not one to believe in love.

"I very much think it can, my lady," he replied.

"So we have an agreement?" Her eyebrows flew up. "I will remain on as long as we get to the bottom of what's bothering our servants."

"We have an agreement." He grinned. "Be it a nudge toward or away from one another."

"Fabulous." She eyed the crowd below. "Then a few more days it is."

He had never heard sweeter words and vowed to make every moment count, starting with their entrance into the ballroom. Or so he had intended until he saw the wary look on her face.

"Are you all right, my lady?" He thanked a servant who delivered drinks. "You have grown quite pale."

"I am." Prudence took in the couples swirling by on the dance floor. "This is just…" She glanced at him uneasily. "It matters not."

"It matters entirely." He kept his arm wrapped with hers lest she swoon. "Would you prefer to leave? We do not need to—"

"No." She inhaled deeply, squared her shoulders, and sipped from her champagne flute. "It is high time I face this again. That I see it in the here and now rather than what it once was."

While curious what she meant, he nodded, sipped his own champagne, and let her go on if she so chose. Hoped she would. That she began to understand the only way beyond her past was through it. By remembering it, then letting it go.

And it just so happened she did.

"You see, balls like this became much dreaded as my marriage went on," she said softly. While some might say the claret they enjoyed while touring had loosened her tongue, he knew better. Deep down, she needed to release this anguish and felt comfortable enough to do so with him. "I came to dread seeing my late husband dance with others because I knew…"

She need not say what she knew. He understood.

"I thought the heartbreak was the worst part," she continued. "But it turned out the embarrassment was far worse. False friends gossiped and pitied me from behind their fans. Or perhaps they thought me a fool as there was a great deal of laughter too."

He could just imagine how that must have felt. How it must have been knowing many of those women had likely bedded her husband. Something she need not say, but he saw on her face. In her eyes. A pain that came and went so quickly one had to be observant to catch it.

"Then might you dance with me instead of watching him dance with others?" He knew it was risky, but he set aside their drinks, bowed from the waist, and held out his hand. Spoke softly lest anyone overhear him. "Might you dance on your terms without others looking down on you? Pitying you? Because you are not to be pitied, Lady Barrington." He shook his head. "Not then and certainly not now."

She glanced from his hand to his face, not with fear but something akin to interest. Perhaps even determination. While he sensed she wanted to distance herself from this as much as he had wanted to distance himself from Elizabeth's pianoforte, it seemed she was braver in the face of change than he because she slipped her hand into his. Better still, he could tell by the ease on her face she had not done it out of obligation to propriety but because she truly wanted to conquer her past.

While the music had initially been livelier, he could not help but note that the band switched to a waltz too swiftly to be a coincidence. To that end, he had little choice but to pull her close and swirl her onto the dance floor.

No choice but to lose himself in a way he never expected.

# Chapter Nine

A s Jacob swirled Prudence into a waltz that almost felt otherworldly, she finally understood what women meant when they claimed their feet never touched the floor upon dancing with a man. Where moments before, she had been painfully aware of everyone and lost in bad memories, everything vanished when in his arms. When lost in his eyes. Because it very much felt that way. As though she fell headfirst into Jacob's chocolate, near-obsidian gaze. Tumbled until he caught her, and she floated.

As if her feet no longer touched the ground.

She had not danced in far too long and thought she would miss a step or two but did the opposite. Whether because he was an excellent dancer and she trusted his lead, or because being with him lent her confidence, she sailed over the floor. *They* sailed as if they had been dancing together all their lives.

Though part of her was tempted to look at all those tittering women from her past hiding behind their fans, she could not pull her gaze from Jacob's face if she tried. Could not glare into the past if she wanted to. Rather, she was completely immersed in the present. Aware only of his heat so close. The strength of his strong, graceful body but inches away.

It seemed he wanted to say something, perhaps reassure her all was well, but he appeared as incapable of speaking as her. As caught up in the moment. Entrenched in something that felt nowhere near platonic. Nowhere near where she had been determined to keep things.

"Nor should they be, dear sister," Grace would say, her heart in her eyes. "Not when a man makes you feel like this. Because this is everything. What you deserve. What you have long deserved."

"While that might be true," her youngest sister, Abby, would argue, "Prudence has every reason to be wary. To keep things platonic with the Lord of Argyll." She could almost see Abby notch her chin. "I know, too, considering my own loveless marriage. The prison it often feels like." Her brows would shoot up. "So I say, why would anyone who suffered such seek anything but freedom and perhaps even adventure after that?"

Abby would make a good point, too. One Prudence should keep firmly at the forefront of her mind when it came to Jacob. And she tried, she really did, but it felt more and more impossible as they danced. Everything about him drew her in. Not just now, either, but every moment since she first walked downstairs.

From the second their gazes locked, she knew her time with him was nowhere near over. That in mind, she needed to rally her courage and apologize at last. For all of it. Not just incidents earlier today but for those from years ago. For causing him such trouble not just in society but in his marriage, because surely she must have. Truth be told, she owed him more of an apology than she had already given, and she fully intended to offer it in time.

Because there *would* be time.

She would see to it because she enjoyed his company immensely. Enough that wherever fate took her next, she would want him in her life. She could not say to what extent, only that he was undoubtedly going to be her first real friend outside of her sisters.

As it happened, they did not just dance one waltz, but three in a row hardly realizing it. Eventually, however, they agreed refreshments were in order and retired to the adjoining room, where Maude waved them over with a wide smile. She stood with Lady Campbell, who smiled in turn.

"Oh, how divine you two looked dancing together." Maude beamed at them. "I could hardly take my eyes off of you when I was in the ballroom."

"Lady Barrington is a splendid dancer." A telling sparkle lit Jacob's eyes when he looked at her. "It truly was my pleasure, my lady."

"Thank you, Your Grace." She warmed beneath his fond regard and the desire she swore flashed in his obsidian gaze. Desire that made her bold, indeed. "We will have to dance again before the night is over."

His smile never wavered. "Nothing would make me happier."

He was about to go on when he was summoned to join several gentlemen, without doubt, to talk business. But not before he murmured in her ear that he would seek her out later and resume spending time with her. Something about the look in his eyes made her suspect he would prefer that time be spent alone. Or perhaps that was her own wanton response to the way his warm breath felt against her skin and the shivers of awareness that had raced through her.

"It seems I am needed elsewhere at the moment as well," Maude said. "I will catch up with you again soon enough, sister." She smiled between Lady Campbell and Prudence. "I am sure Lady Campbell would enjoy your company until I return."

Maude was up to something again. She was certain of it.

"I would very much enjoy Lady Barrington's company." Lady Campbell smiled at Prudence as they took flutes of champagne off the tray of a passing server. "Might we stroll? This castle is spacious enough we need not remain in such a busy room."

"That would be lovely, Lady Campbell." Yet she suspected there was more to it and that in some small way, she was being evaluated and perhaps even held up against Jacob's late wife.

"I insist you call me Emma when we are alone or with good friends," Lady Campbell said. "For I do so hope we become dear friends."

She did? Whatever for? But she supposed she must be polite. Not just that, but the idea of making new friends was not so terribly awful. She would have to see how things went with Emma. What kind of person she was.

"That would be lovely." She met Emma's smile. "Though I am not sure how often I will be in Scotland."

"Well, I can only hope often enough," Emma said bluntly. "For it does my heart good to see the Duke of Argyll so happy again."

"Is he not usually happy, then?" While days ago, she would have thought the woman far too forthright, it seemed Jacob preferred to keep such company. Moreover, having such an honest conversation with another woman made it feel like one more bar had fallen from her cage. Not just that, but she was curious about what Emma had to say. "He has struck me as content thus far."

"Content, yes." Emma's brows pinched as they made their way down a hallway of portraits she had not been down before. "Happy? I would say not, however much he tries to convince me otherwise."

"You speak rather plainly about him, considering you have only just met me," Prudence could not help but point out. "Would he approve of such?"

"I think, in your case, he rather might." More astute than anticipated, Emma considered her. "Either way, I admire your need to protect him despite your own curiosity." She cocked her head and spoke more plainly still. "Because you *are* curious, are you not, Lady Barrington? Perhaps not as curious about me anymore, but very much so about the duke."

She nearly denied it but found Emma's level of honesty preferable to the usual verbal dance of half-truths and outright lies of which those of their society were so adept.

"I will admit I was curious about you earlier today but regret to confess it was for all the wrong reasons." She nodded graciously. "So, yes, it is safe to say my curiosity now lies solely in the Duke of Argyll."

"I cannot tell you how glad I am to hear that." Emma linked arms with Prudence as they strolled. "Yet still, I would like you to know me a tad better before divulging more about our dear duke if you would not mind?"

"I would not." She sipped her champagne and swallowed back a flash of fear that, despite all she had learned today, Emma secretly pined for him. "Do tell."

It turned out the things Emma shared really were about herself. From her upbringing to how she met her first husband when she debuted into the ton. How he had passed quite suddenly, and she found herself adrift.

"However briefly, we shared an amiable few years together," she went on. "When he passed, I felt off-kilter, for lack of a better way to put it. Unsure how to go about things since I was no longer in those first few years of blooming youth."

"Yet you are so very lovely." Prudence took in her soft, golden curls and flawless skin. "And still quite young, so undoubtedly young then."

"To other eyes, perhaps." Emma shrugged. "But it took some time to see what they saw. To rejoin society with confidence, whether I remarried or not."

"Ah." She saw where this was going and, in the spirit of honesty, said as much. "You assume because I wore this dress tonight that I am seeing my way through the same struggles."

"Are you not?"

"I suppose I am," she said. "Though, if I were to be truthful, I did not choose to wear this gown of my own volition."

Emma's brow perked. "No?"

"No." She narrowed her eyes. "But I suspect you already knew that."

"I may have," Emma confessed. "Though I hazard to say, however unique the circumstances, you did, in the end, wear it of your own volition."

She could see why Jacob and Emma got along so well. They were equally entertaining.

"I suppose you could say I did." Because she had.

"Why?"

"I think you know why," she said before she could stop herself.

Emma eyed her with curiosity. "Was it all for him, then?"

She nearly replied *yes* because a great deal of it had been for Jacob, but then she remembered how she first felt when she looked in the mirror, and then the sensation that another few bars in her cage had fallen away.

"No, it was not all for him." She offered Emma a small smile. "It was for me as well. Quite a bit for me, actually."

"Good." Emma smiled as well. Emma met her smile. "Because that is truly the best place to start, Lady Barrington."

"Call me Prudence." She surprised herself by saying it but was glad she did. Another bar was removed, she supposed. It was a leap she was not ready to take with Jacob, but Emma was a good start.

Emma's smile grew. "Prudence, it is." She sipped her champagne and admired Prudence's dress. "I must say, for a first leap back into the beast of proper society, you did so stunningly."

"I think we both know I can thank my sister for that."

"We can thank her for providing it." Emma gave her a look. "But only you can be thanked for actually wearing it." She stopped and gestured at a nearby painting. "And again, dress or no, for putting a smile like that on our duke's face once more."

Her breath caught when she looked at the portrait of Jacob and a beautiful woman. He wore a blue and green checkered tartan, and she a matching dress. While certainly a striking pair, it was their happiness that really captured the viewer.

His happiness, most of all.

"My cousin, Lady Elizabeth, was a truly lovely person." Emma's voice caught with emotion. "I suppose you could say her gift was helping others find the sort of happiness she naturally possessed. She certainly did so with Jacob. Much-needed happiness, to be sure."

While tempted to ask why it was much needed, she would rather have him tell her in good time if he so chose.

"It is a stunning portrait." Without understanding quite why she was so touched by the painting, she blinked back tears. "They clearly shared a great love."

"They did." Emma's gaze drifted to Prudence and held for a moment. "And that does not bother you, does it?"

"Not in the least." She remained as blunt as Emma. "Did you intend such when you walked me this way so that I might see it?"

Because she clearly had.

"No, but I confess I was interested in how you might react to it." Her gaze softened. "I must admit, I did not expect tears."

"Any more than I." She blinked them away the best she could. "My apologies."

"Whatever for?" Emma glanced from the portrait to Prudence. "Though I will admit to being curious as to what part of the picture touches you most."

"Every part." Her gaze drifted to the portrait again. "The happiness and love they found together. The light in her eyes and warmth in his smile. The family they would share together." She swallowed back a lump in her throat. "A future that was everything she thought it would be. A man who remained true to who he seemed to be at the beginning. Whose eyes never strayed. Whose love never wavered…"

Silence fell as she trailed off.

"Well, you do have it all quite right." Emma blinked back tears of her own. "Very astute of you." Warm appreciation lit her gaze as they continued strolling. "Might you find the same, for I suspect you deserve it."

"Do I?" she wondered softly, more saddened than ever that she had slandered a man who had so clearly adored his wife.

"I would say you very much do," Emma said. "And it is clear Jacob feels the same, or he would not have befriended you."

She was not sure what to make of that. Did Emma mean he befriended her to help her find love again? For that was a rather strange thing to do for anyone. Or did she imply he had befriended her because he was attracted to her? That perhaps he drew some similarities between her and his late wife and hoped to court her despite what she had done to him years ago?

While tempted to be honest and ask, she could not seem to do it for no other reason than she feared the answer.

Fortunately, friends of Emma's soon joined them, so she was spared from having to look at her feelings too closely. They were emotions far too new to be trusted. Instead, she spent the next few hours *enjoying* people rather than suffering through them. Much to her astonishment, she even enjoyed Maude's company. The good Lord knew she loved her sister but had never expected to actually find her improper and unorthodox ways charming.

"I do hope you will forgive me for the dress mishap," Maude said at one point, her eyes far too merry for a proper apology. "I only meant to see your belongings well-prepared for your upcoming travels."

"No doubt you did." Yet she could not seem to find it in herself to be put off anymore. "I can only hope my night rail, at the very least, makes a reappearance."

"One must hope," Maude echoed with a rather wicked gleam in her eyes.

Prudence nearly said going without a night rail was taking it a step too far but bit her tongue when Jacob rejoined her. After that, she could care less about bedtime attire, especially when the two of them picked up their conversation flawlessly and exactly where they had left off. Only then did it occur to her she had not scanned the room for him once like she used to look for her late husband. Never worried what mischief he might be up to.

Then again, Jacob was not her husband or even courting her, so he need not be scrutinized. Nor were there worries about him behaving in a certain way. Even if he were courting her, she now knew there was nothing to fear. He was not the man her husband had been. Nowhere near it, for that matter. It was an exhilarating thought and made her heart warm and even—perhaps—happy.

"You seem to be enjoying yourself, my lady," he said at one juncture, never allowing her off his arm. "It is good to see."

"I am," she admitted, smiling at others when they smiled at her. "Very much so."

They talked a great deal but mostly danced, and she loved every minute of it. Adored the way they moved together when waltzing or the chats they had during less formal dances. It was the most time she had ever spent on a dance floor, and she found herself quite weary when the evening wound down.

Jacob held out his elbow. "Might I walk you to your room, my lady?"

Her heart leapt a little as she slipped her arm into his. "I would like that, Your Grace."

While she knew there was nothing untoward about him escorting her to her bed chambers, her heart beat faster than usual the whole way up. The portraits that seemed so fascinating earlier dulled in comparison to the warmth of his arm. To the rich timbre of his voice as they continued chatting.

"I must admit, I loathe seeing this night come to an end," he said when they arrived at her door. "More so that I could not enjoy your company for its entirety."

While uncharacteristically tempted to gush that she felt the same, she had actually appreciated her moments alone almost as much as those with him. The newfound sense of freedom she had felt being on her own. The confidence she had found within it.

So, quite liking the way Emma went about things, she remained truthful and friendly because she thought it best for now. Better that they kept things platonic, lest she fall into his arms and do something she regretted. Had to think that way. "While I missed our conversations in your absence, it was truly a lovely evening. One I hope we can repeat."

"I would like nothing more, my lady."

Her heart leapt into her throat, and heat flared under her skin when he leaned in slowly and kissed her cheek. His lips hovered so close to hers before he pulled away that she feared he might kiss her on the mouth. Or was it hope she felt when her knees grew weak? A desperate yearning that he took matters out of her hands and closed his mouth over hers? Kiss her in a way she had hoped her late husband would have, at least at the beginning of their marriage?

He did not, though, and despite wanting his lips on hers, she was grateful when he bid her goodnight. That he let their wonderful night stand as it was. Agnus had not come up yet to help her undress, and she was grateful for it. Thankful for a few moments alone so she could open her balcony doors and step out into the refreshingly cool air.

It was the first time she had dared to step out there since arriving, and she could not help but wonder what she had been waiting for. She cared not for the chill but let her shawl fall away. Turned her face up to the moon as though warming it in the sun. Felt it wash over her and tear away yet one more bar from her gilded cage.

She had never expected to feel like this again. But then, had she felt this way to begin with? Before being presented at her debutante ball years ago? Before going into the world with such a naïve outlook? Before thinking that love was destined? That the world could be changed because she merely wished it?

Now she knew otherwise, and for the first time in ages, she was not so bitter about it. She had begun seeing things for what they were, while at the same time realizing there was hope to be had. That there were kind people out there, and especially that the world was not black, white, or the leaden grey it had become.

Rather it was quite vibrant, and the next few days proved that.

In fact, the next few days showed her more than she ever dared imagine.

# Chapter Ten

I T TOOK EVERYTHING in Jacob not to close his lips over Prudence's when he escorted her to her room. Every time he saw her, he thought it impossible she could be lovelier, but somehow upon returning after seeing to business earlier, she seemed changed once again. Utterly transformed once more when she bypassed a mere smile and outright laughed at something Emma had said.

She was so transformed that he had stood off for a bit so he could simply admire her. Watch her laugh and be happy. Thrive in the capable hands of the MacLauchlins and Campbells. Because she could have no more genuine acquaintances nor better friends.

To say things were going as he had hoped with Prudence was an understatement. She was finding her way back to herself far more quickly than the lasses he had been with before when he had helped them along until they amiably returned down their own paths.

While he was glad Prudence had found her way out from beneath her late husband's tyranny so quickly, he could not help but wonder...*did* she need romance to find her way back to herself? Or was Blake right, and perhaps it would be poor of him to take things any further?

It was a conundrum he grappled with when he'd nearly kissed her plush lips. However difficult it might be, he decided until he figured things out, it was best to keep things chaste between them. So over the next few days he continued to keep things platonic and enjoyed himself more than he had in a long time.

"Well, it seems I owe you yet another apology, Your Grace," Prudence said. They had just come from mass at church and stood in one of the two buildings he had wanted to show her days ago. She gazed around at nothing more than crumbling walls, dinge, and dust. "This is outstanding." Seeing something most lasses would not, she shook her head in awe. "I can just imagine how it looked when wounded soldiers were brought in here during wartime. What a relief it must have been to find sanctuary and medical care."

Ironically, considering that their initial conversation was about the Jacobite Rising, this particular building had played a crucial part during that time for those wounded in battle and a part of Scottish history he would see resurrected so all might come here and remember the sacrifices that had been made. And especially, how Scots had stood by their countrymen until the bitter end.

"Soon enough, I will walk you in here, and you will see it as it once was." Envisioning all the possibilities, he eyed the place. "It will be something. I promise you that."

"And I shall hold you to your word." She smiled as they linked arms and walked out. "For I would very much like to see Scotland brought back to its former glory."

"Would you really?" He could not help but return her smile. "After all, mere days ago, you dreaded stepping foot in this 'horrid' country."

It seemed they had done nothing but talk, smile, and laugh together for the better part of three days, so he knew he could tease her without repercussions. Knew he could be blatantly honest, if he so wished, because she had urged him to do just that.

"Actually, it has been the better part of a week." Her smile faded, and she grew serious. "But I can say, with all honesty, my preconceived notions about your country were wrong. Scotland and its people have proven..." she seemed to struggle with emotion before continuing, "most gracious and quite wonderful."

He reflected on the past few days and the changes that had come about.

UPON HEARING FROM Emma that Prudence had been willing to call her by her given name, he had since persisted in her calling him Jacob, but she refused. Where it had clearly been out of decorum at the start, it felt more personal now. As if she were determined not to cross that boundary because it might land her in his bed.

If only he were that lucky.

While he had questioned how he should handle things when he kissed her on the cheek nights before, as time went on, he only desired one thing. Thought endlessly about one subject.

Her in his bed and nowhere else.

Unfortunately, he suspected Prudence was not quite there. More alarming, if she did get there, she might not stay. How could she when it became clear she quite liked the independence she had found?

"Can you blame her?" Emma had asked on their morning stroll. He hoped Prudence might appear, but she had not. "If the rumors hold true, Lady Barrington was terribly repressed. So I see nothing wrong with her spreading her wings a wee bit, my dear." She had been clear where she stood, and it was very much in Prudence's corner. "And I would think you nothing but her staunch supporter? Nothing but her stalwart defender when it comes to making her way back to happiness and into another man's arms." She had considered him curiously. "Was that not your purpose from the start?"

"It was and is." Yet the words had felt awkward on his

tongue. "Prudence deserves happiness no matter what it takes."

"She does." Emma had narrowed her eyes as though not quite sure she liked that *no matter what it takes* part. "To that end, I might be able to help her in ways you cannot."

He had asked her what she meant, but she offered no reply other than to say it was in Prudence's best interest. To his mind, which meant her returning to Argyll with him and becoming his lover until his last dying breath. It was something he had never asked of another. Outside of his late wife, the thought never even crossed his mind, and he was not sure what to make of it other than he felt it. Wanted it. Yet he got the distinct impression Emma intended to stand in his way.

More so, that Prudence was not so ripe for the taking.

Which, as he watched her blossom, was very much as it should be. Not only was she beautiful but intelligent, and she deserved the opportunity to go her own way. Going the way he himself had hoped she would when he first learned she would be visiting MacLauchlin Castle.

"Your Grace?" Prudence drew him back to the present. "Are you well?"

A very good question. Was he? It was impossible to know.

"Aye." He met her smile. "Very well, my lady."

Her smile faltered, and she slowed. "Are you sure?"

They might not have known each other long, but she had an uncanny way of seeing things others could not. Emotions he learned to mask when he became a duke. When he had to present himself in a certain way, no matter what he might be feeling.

"I am sure." He said what made sense and the truth in more ways than one. "Though I admit it saddens me, I must leave tomorrow."

"As does it me." Prudence smiled and nudged him a little, clearly trying to improve his mood. "But we will correspond, yes?" She gave him a look much like he had given her days before when he said nearly the same thing. "For I will grow fatally bored the minute I do not hear from you."

Despite his ever-encroaching sadness, he could not help but tease back with how she had replied in turn. "Not the very second?"

"Indeed, you might be right about that." She tilted her head in thought before her eyes brightened. "Then perhaps we should start straight away?"

"Do share."

"Well, why not write each other a letter this very night?" she suggested. "Then we can have my maid and your valet deliver them to us so we might continue communicating right after you depart?"

"Ah, yes, those two." He grinned and narrowed his eyes in contemplation. "Do we dare, given parlay failed, and they are now at war?"

As implied, things had gone from bad to worse below stairs, and their servants' bickering and roaring at each other might very well go down in MacLauchlin Castle history. That was according to gossiping staff, of course, because neither Agnus nor Donal admitted to such. As far as either disclosed, their dealings with one another had been most cordial and businesslike. Most proper as their stations dictated.

"I think we *should* entrust them with our first official correspondence." Prudence nodded once. "May they risk our eternal wrath otherwise."

He chuckled at her mimicking one of the many medieval quotes he had shared during their ongoing tour of the castle over the past few days. They had covered nearly every inch but the room in which Elizabeth's pianoforte resided. To be expected, he continued enjoying her company immensely and to the point he had grown desperate for the next time he would see her, and they recommenced. How could he not want to see her, with her limitless curiosity? Her remarkable thirst for learning?

"Then risk of our eternal wrath it is because I think your idea splendid," he said. "We shall start our correspondence straight away lest you or I grow fatally bored within seconds of being apart."

"Very good." Her smile only grew. "Would it be wrong to admit I am already penning it in my mind?"

"Not at all," he assured. "As I am doing the same, my lady."

He was, too. Likely had been in some small way since the moment she arrived at MacLauchlin Castle. Had she as well? Did she feel the same way he did despite such a short courtship? No, not a courtship, he reminded himself once again. Theirs was anything but. Rather it was the start of what he knew would be a lifelong friendship and perhaps—hopefully—even more.

It seemed an unspoken thing that they found each other at every opportunity. That they were fast friends everyone expected to see together. They knew gossip was about, and everyone thought them courting. So he supposed, in their own way, they went with it. Him, because he would be by no one else's side. Her, perhaps, to keep free of would-be suitors so she might simply enjoy herself.

"Ah, the bagpipes are playing." She turned an especially radiant smile his way. "Might we go listen to them again?"

If he did not hear her crisp English accent, he might think her a Scot for the way she was drawn to the pipes. For how she seemed adrift in their sound every bit as much as she was the first day when he dared not approach. He had since asked her what she heard when she listened to them, and she responded with one succinct word. One that caught him off guard but truly did sum it all up.

*Heart.*

She heard *heart* in the pipes, and he understood that. Had always felt the same. What he could never have anticipated was the same prudish Englishwoman who had tried to ruin his good name years before, hearing the same. Who felt it so strongly he knew better than to chat when they came upon the man playing the pipes. Which was fine, as he much preferred watching her out of the corner of his eye, especially how she appeared to lose herself in the music.

He would have to make sure bagpipes were playing whenever they reunited. Because they would be reuniting and often. Always if he could convince her to…what? He still had not figured out that part. All he knew was the idea of letters every so often sounded pitiful. Depressing. Why write when he could see her? Be around her? Enjoy her wonder at the world?

For all they had talked, there was still much left to discuss. Things they had not broached. Her time with her husband. His time with his wife. But was any of that really necessary? Somehow he sensed it might be before all was said and done. That her relationship with her husband could very well be part of what ultimately kept her away if they did not open up fully to one another, even as friends.

"A pint of ale, Your Grace?" a kindly old vender asked in passing. He offered Prudence a fairly toothless grin. "My lady?"

He was about to say *nay*, but it seemed Prudence decided to dive headfirst into things she had turned away even a day ago.

"That would be lovely." She took the mug handed to her and smiled warmly, saying two simple words she would never have said before. "Thank you."

"Aye, my lady." When the old man seemed unable to stop beaming at Prudence, Jacob handed him enough to cover the cost of two ales, sure to grab the other mug before the smitten vendor wandered off.

"Are you quite certain about this?" He looked at Prudence's ale, then perked a brow at her. "When you were holy against it even yesterday?"

"I was because supposedly it is strong." She sniffed it and flinched before she nodded once firmly. "Therefore, I will sip it so I might have a taste of good Scottish ale, as you call it."

"Well, then, Lady Barrington." He tapped his mug against hers. "Here is to an adventurous Englishwoman drinking good Scottish ale."

"Here, here." Clearly doing her best not to scrunch her nose, she took a dainty sip, only to narrow her eyes.

"Well, what do you think?"

"I am not sure." She took another dainty sip, only this time less squeamishly. "Other than…"

He chuckled when she sniffed it again, then took one more sip. "Other than what, my lady?"

She seemed to give it a great deal of thought before she relented. "In truth, it is not nearly as foul tasting as the scent implies."

He tapped his mug against hers again and said the only thing that came to mind. What seemed to make perfect sense. "Then, I do believe you would make a proper Scotswoman, Lady Barrington."

While she said nothing to that, he did not miss the odd look in her eyes before they carried on with their day. What had he seen in that glimpse? Could it be a desire to leave her roots behind and move to Scotland? Mayhap find a new life here? Better still, one where she would be in his bed discreetly every night? One in which he might wake to her beautiful face every morning before she snuck back to wherever?

A fantasy, as it were, that stayed with him the remainder of the day.

What would it be like to have her reside in his castle as a visitor? Be able to bring her to his bed every night? Feel her soft skin against his? See her writhe in pleasure beneath him? Because he would make it his mission to see her feel all the pleasure she had been long denied. Make her cry out in ecstasy until the wee hours of the morn.

"What is that faraway look in your eyes, dear friend?" Emma said later on as they stood in front of the fire in the great hall. Her knowing gaze drifted up a staircase Prudence had yet to come down. "It is new and often, and I quite like it."

He blinked, startled out of his reverie but understanding, as always, that Emma was no fool. "I imagine it is my increasing desire for Lady Barrington's company."

"Quite right." Emma nodded in approval. "And for that, I

applaud you, Jacob. She is a rare gem."

The way she said it caught his attention. "I am not sure I have ever heard you say that about anyone but Elizabeth."

"Because I have not nor will I likely ever again." She peered up the stairs as if she could look into a future he could not. "So perhaps now more than ever, you might keep in mind, because I know you see it yourself, that Prudence is well on her way to recovery. She has done very well distancing herself from her life in England in little time and begun a healing process we both know she needed."

Again, she insinuated he was no longer needed in certain regards. Romance was not the best option.

"I understand," he said gruffly. "Friendship truly is the best option at this point."

"Aye." Emma surprised him when she rested a hand on his arm and gazed at him in a way she never quite had before. "Not for her sake, but for yours, Jacob. At least, for now."

He frowned, but it was lost on her as she drifted into the crowd. Whatever did she mean? Because it sounded quite serious. Yet it meant little the moment he spied Prudence coming downstairs in yet another lovely gown. It seemed the various new dresses her sister had originally provided reappeared in her armoire after that first night. Better still, she had decided to wear them. While miffed her sister had left her with one dress at the start, she told him on the sly that she was grateful.

"Why?" he asked.

She'd thought about it a moment before answering frankly. "Because it gave me no choice but to wear something else. To step out of dresses that were no different than my mourning clothes."

He sensed she wanted to say more but held back. But then, that was their way. They might talk endlessly about history and architecture and other interesting topics, but when it came to the things that mattered most, neither were much ready for that. Why would they be when they had only just become friends?

Only just started to get to know each other?

As he was wont to do every time he saw her come down those stairs, he met her at the bottom. And as everyone seemed to understand, the crowd parted that he might do so. This evening she wore a lovely blue gown that made her eyes all that much more vibrant.

"Your Grace," she said with a warm smile as she slipped her arm into his.

"My lady," he replied, helpless to do anything but offer her an equally warm smile. "You look ravishing as always."

She might blush prettily, but her confidence was much improved. So said the way she nodded graciously and thanked him without ever losing eye contact.

As usual, they dined together and then made their way about the much-toned-down celebrations. This was the eve of a religious holiday, so the crowd was considerably thinned.

"I must say, I prefer it like this," she said softly, almost reverently, as they made their way down the same candlelit hallway they had that first night. "It feels more suited to the castle. As though it breathes a sigh of relief for the privacy."

"It does feel that way." He adored the way she saw things. "And can you blame it?"

"Not in the slightest." She inhaled deeply as if breathing in the castle itself. "I find when it is like this, I can better imagine all those that walked its halls before us. Their timeless tales."

"And what sort of tales would they be?"

"From what I have learned of Scotland thus far, I would say stories of sacrifice, heartache, and loss." Her gaze grew a little dreamy. "But of love and new beginnings, too. Your Scots persevere. Stand strong despite so much." Her gaze wandered over the numerous ancestors gazing down at them. "Much like the MacLauchlin brothers. Three scoundrels who were at the heart of so much. Such a wonderful legacy."

"There ye go with that word scoundrel again, lassie," he teased but fully agreed. "Aye, Laird Teagan and his brothers were at the heart of much. All you see today. And the MacLauchlins couldnae be more thankful."

"I like it when you do that," she murmured.

"What?"

"Speak medieval." She offered the sort of soft smile he wanted to wake up to every morning. "And voice the brogue natural to you rather than the aristocratic version best suited in surroundings you have no choice but to tolerate."

"Have you gathered all that then?" he said gruffly, more taken by her by the moment if such were possible.

She was about to respond when piano music drifted down the hall. Sweet music that lulled and saddened him all at once and threatened old memories.

"I should retire." Prudence squeezed his hand and gave him a reassuring, supportive look. "And you should go on. Be with your late wife. Remember her."

He should. Meant to. Yet he could not seem to move forward.

"I let her go years ago," he said. "But somehow her piano returning to this castle...."

"I know." She looked from the direction of the music back to him, tentatively. "Would you like me to accompany you or—"

"Aye," he said impulsively but meant it. He squeezed her hand in return. "I would verra much like that."

So she did and it proved that he had felt when he first danced with her paled in comparison to how she was about to make him feel. Especially when she was the last person he should be thinking about at such a time.

# Chapter Eleven

P RUDENCE'S HEART WENT out to Jacob as they continued down the hall toward the sound of Elizabeth's piano. She had been prepared to leave him be, but he wanted her with him, so here she was, more terrified than she could ever remember being.

Should she be here? Did she belong? What was she doing?

While uncertainties nagged at her initially, the sadness on his face made her snap out of her own trepidation and instead be the friend he needed. This was not about her and what they may or may not feel for one another. This was about the duke and the woman who had meant a great deal to him and about being confronted with her memory in a castle that belonged to her kin.

A memory elicited by the piano he had likely watched his wife play.

So she rallied forth every bit of strength she could for him and kept a supportive arm linked with his when they entered the room. She remained supportive as the few seated in the dimly lit room enjoying the music nodded as they sat. While decorum said they should not touch, she cared not and held his hand as he stared at the piano as if lost in memory. Decorum, in this case, mattered little to her at the moment.

She remained silent and listened, letting the sound fill her every bit as much as the bagpipes. How could she not when it was every bit as beautiful? Told its own tale. Much like the portrait of Jacob and Elizabeth, there was passion in it and deep, untouchable love. Timeless notes that would always remain in its keys.

They sat there for a time listening, Jacob in his own world, she in hers, imagining the love he had shared with his wife. She wasn't jealous of it but appreciative, wishing she had found such a thing and oddly—considering how only until recently she'd held him in ill-regard—grateful that he had found it. Eventually, he squeezed her hand again, letting her know he was all right and ready to press on. So they made their way back into the hallway.

"Thank you for that, my lady," he said softly. "I appreciate it more than you know."

"Of course," she said. "And thank you for allowing me to join you. The music was lovely. Your late wife's piano is a grand instrument, indeed. I could imagine her playing it. The loving looks you two must have shared when she did."

"We did." He stopped walking, turned to her and grew most serious. "But that love is in the past now. It has been for some time." His voice dropped an octave and his gaze lingered on her face. "Despite what you just witnessed, it is important that you understand that. Hearing her piano played in this castle again offered a sense of closure, I suppose. A final goodbye to someone beloved."

"Then I am glad you were able to do so." There could be no mistaking the way he looked at her now. "That I was able to join you in saying goodbye."

"As was I." She got the distinct impression he struggled to say one thing but said another instead. "I find I could use a spot of fresh air. Care to join me?"

"I would like nothing more." Anything to spend more time with him before they retired for the evening and said their own goodbye in the morning.

As it turned out, even though he had taken her there before, they retrieved their coats and returned to the battlements. To be expected, they were very much alone. While torches had been lit to keep the ambiance of the castle, the walkway was quite dark. Even though a window-encased room had been built up here more recently to allow people to enjoy the view when it grew cold, they stood outside.

"It is as lovely here in the evening as it was during the day." She gazed at the moon-swept countryside. "Once again, I can only imagine what it was like hundreds of years ago standing guard up here. How difficult it must have been trying to spy enemies approaching in the darkness."

"Difficult indeed." He led her to an especially dark area. "Torches would have been diminished during times of higher threat so guardsmen could not be seen. And if one had no choice but to light a torch to help allies find the way, they could see those approaching more easily in spots like this without the glare of firelight."

"To be sure." She might be taking in her surroundings, but she was wholly aware of how close he stood. How secluded the spot.

"The key, of course," he turned her a little, stood behind her, and pointed toward the drawbridge, "is to position yourself just so and keep a close eye on the tree line beyond the bridge torches. That is where you would most likely see movement first."

She meant to reply but found her voice useless at his proximity. At the feel of his warmth at her back. How his arm felt when it came around her waist to keep her steady against the wind shear. Being in his embrace on the dance floor was one thing. This, quite another. Her body thrummed in anticipation. A familiar ache unique to him blossomed between her thighs.

"Jacob," she whispered, using his name for the first time. When she glanced over her shoulder, it was to find his eyes on her rather than the countryside. There was no missing his desire when his gaze dropped to her mouth.

She should stop this if she meant to keep their friendship intact, but she was helpless to pull away when he turned her in his arms and cupped her cheek tenderly. Helpless to do anything but allow his lips to close over hers. To lose herself in a kiss so entirely different than any her late husband had given her.

While gentle at first, it became more insistent when his tongue slipped into her mouth. She had never experienced such but very much liked it and met his tongue with hers. After that, everything but him and how he made her feel faded away, to the extent she hardly realized he had moved them into the glass-encased room.

A dwindling fire crackled on the hearth, allowing more darkness than light so no one could see when he backed her up against a wall. Nobody saw how hungry their kisses grew. They were in their own little oasis where passion could hide, and sin could flourish. Because it felt that way. Sinful and daring as his warm hand cupped the back of her neck, and he pulled her against him.

She could not help a groan when the dull throb between her thighs became a raging ache. When she felt the hard length he pressed against her.

In turn, she pressed back. Wanted more. Part of her knew it was far too fast, and they should be married, but another, more wanton part, wanted it anyway.

Wanted it without marriage and free of obligation.

While quite looked down upon by the upper crust, it happened more often than one would think. Widowed women discreetly took lovers. And while she had thought it crude and indecent a week ago, she now saw the appeal. The freedom it would afford to enjoy such and not worry about producing heirs. Rather, by the feel of it, clandestine meetings with men like Jacob were all about pleasure.

So she let herself go when his warm hand rode up under her skirt. Gasped against his lips when his clever fingers found their way between her quivering thighs. He stroked her sensitive flesh, and their kisses intensified. When he slid first one, then two fingers inside her but kept the pad of his thumb on the tiny nub at the apex of her pleasure, breathing much less kissing became impossible.

Her head fell back, and her eyes slid shut at the sensations welling inside her. Glorious pleasure made that much better by the way his breathing grew choppy in her ear, as though he found equal pleasure. By the way he peppered kisses down the side of her neck and groaned in approval when she thrust her hips in rhythm with his fingers. Moved against him like she might if far more than his fingers were inside her.

Her skin grew hotter still as he kept stroking. Gave her no choice but to race toward some unknown pinnacle. Some unvisited wondrous place that freed her of all her inhibitions. Ripped away the last of her mental cage.

Because it would.

She was sure of it.

Almost as if the mere thought of such freedom in Jacob's embrace pushed her over the edge, a strange sort of ecstasy tore through her. She cried out and stiffened before she shuddered, and a glorious rush washed over her. Thank goodness he held her up because her legs became useless.

When she finally managed to open her eyes, he watched her as if enraptured. As though he had never seen anything so arousing. While she thought he would come between her thighs and make love to her like he so clearly wanted to, he cupped her cheek and whispered hoarsely, "No," as if reading her mind. Or, very likely, reading her longing to experience him that way no matter how wondrous he had just made her feel.

"But—"

"No." He put a finger to her lips and shook his head. "Not here. Not like this." When she went to argue again because she had never wanted anything so much, he made things clear. "I will have you. We will have each other. But it will not be against a cold stone wall in a chilly chamber where anyone could happen upon us at any moment." He brushed the pad of his thumb over her lower lip and clenched his jaw as if it took a great deal of strength to hold back. "You will come to my castle in Argyll as my guest. Then—and only then—will I make love to you in a way befitting you."

"Befitting me?" She was not sure what to make of that statement other than it did not sit quite right. "I might be wrong, but are you saying it would befit me to come to your castle and become your lover rather than your wife?" Before he could reply, she wiggled out of his embrace, glad that her legs seemed to work again. "Not that I have any interest in remarrying, mind you, but is your proposal not offensive to a woman of my stature? Of *any* stature, for that matter?"

"You misunderstand." Jacob sighed and raked a hand through his hair. "I meant no offense." He reeled her back into his arms and tilted her chin until she had no choice but to look at him. "I do not desire marriage either, but I *do* want you near me. Want to see you more often than mere sporadic visits. To talk with you daily. Hear your voice rather than read your words. See you smile. Laugh when you laugh."

While she had been waiting for the perfect time to tell him her news, it seemed unfortunate, rather than opportune, that this was it. Had to be.

"Yet I am afraid you will not, Your Grace. At least not as frequently as you might like," she said. "Upon Lady Campbell's offer, I have decided to sell my late husband's home in Mayfair and purchase her manor in Dalness."

He seemed caught unaware by that, and she could not tell whether in a good way or not.

"So you mean to remain in Scotland?" he said, stating the obvious.

"I do." Excited despite herself, she could not help but smile. "I find I have quite taken to this country and people, so when Lady Campbell offered, I could not help but accept."

"But of course she did," he murmured.

"Are you disappointed?" she wondered when he seemed saddened.

"Yes and no." His gaze softened on her. "Most certainly disappointed that you will not return to my castle with me as I suspect you would love it." He pressed his lips together for a moment as if biting back emotion before continuing. "But you are right. I should never have asked you to my estate under any other circumstances than with a marriage proposal. That was callous of me. Moreover, you deserve a place of your own. One in which I only ever wish you happiness."

"Thank you," she whispered, touched, lost in the way he looked at her. She cleared her throat and found her voice again. "I can only hope you will visit. That we will remain fast friends."

"I would very much like and expect nothing else, my lady."

"Prudence."

"Prudence," he said softly, cupping her cheek in a way that told her they would be more than friends if he had his way. If she would have him, however discreetly. "You know you will only be a day's ride from me. That I could wake in the morning and be with you by evening."

"Then I will hold you to that." She leaned into his touch. "In return, I would very much like to visit your castle on occasion, as I hear it is quite lovely."

"Lovely, indeed." He searched her eyes. "You will, aye? Visit me as often as I will try to visit you?"

"Yes." Her gaze fell to his lips. How she wanted to kiss him again but knew if she did, she might never stop. That she would fall into his arms once more and perhaps forget all the plans she had for herself. Run to his castle and be anything he wanted. "You have my word."

Before he could reply or kiss her again, she pulled away. "As much as I detest the eve ending, I grow weary and must still write you a letter." She worked at a smile. Tried not to let him see how much she would miss him too. "I can find my way back to my room."

"You will do no such thing." He visibly gathered himself and held out his elbow. "I will escort you there and perhaps see you in the morning before I depart?"

While she should say no because it was bound to be tor-turous, he was her friend, if nothing else, so she agreed.

And it was every bit as difficult as she knew it would be the next morning. However early the hour and despite how few people were about, they could not say what they truly wanted to, so a strained silence settled between them at breakfast.

She knew Emma saw that, too, when she and Lord Campbell joined them. Likely Maude and Lord MacLauchlin as well when they appeared shortly thereafter. All had risen to see Jacob off, and she could not help but wonder if it was for his sake or hers. Either way, she was glad to see them.

Most especially Maude and Emma.

All bid Jacob farewell in the great hall and lingered at the top of the steps outside as Prudence walked him down. While they merely linked elbows, she knew by the way he looked at her he wished for more.

"I will miss you dearly, my lady," he said softly before they reached his carriage. "I trust you received the letter I wrote you last night? The first of many?"

"I did," she said just as softly. "I trust you received mine as well?"

"Aye." Jacob turned to her at the bottom of the stairs but did not touch her lest others wag their tongues any more than she suspected they already did. He started to speak, then stopped as though debating what he wanted to say. As if he wished to say how he truly felt but knew better with his footman standing nearby. "As soon as you are established, I would like to visit." There was no mistaking his worry at her being alone. "To see how you fare, of course. To make sure all is well."

"I would like that, Your Grace." She wanted to touch his cheek. Pull his lips down to hers. Kiss him one last time before they went their separate ways. Instead, she offered a warm smile and hoped he understood the look in her eyes. The desire in her heart. "Very much so."

"Then so it shall be, Lady Barrington." He kissed her cheek

much like he had the first night he walked her to her bedroom door and murmured in her ear, "I will be counting down the days. The very hours."

When he lingered for a moment, she felt it right down to her toes. Felt it between her thighs as though they were back on the battlements again.

"As will I," she whispered because she would. She had even confessed such in her letter because she could not help herself.

When their eyes connected once more, she knew she would find similar words in his letter. That whatever this was between them was well beyond friendship. Some might say that was seen clearly enough last night, but it was more than that.

To the point that when his carriage pulled away, she was grateful Emma appeared on one side of her and Maude, the other. Neither said a word as she swallowed hard and blinked back tears. Rather they linked arms with her, and the three took a stroll.

Nothing was said about Jacob's departure. Instead, they kept the focus on her new home and all she might discover there. How she would make it her own and fall in love with the countryside. How could she not when she had a sneaking suspicion she had already fallen in love with one of its country-men?

Granted, she knew little of love and what it felt like, nor if such a thing were possible so fast, only that when she was finally alone again in her bedroom, she wept. Just like she had the night before when penning his letter. She knew it was foolish but could not help it. The interesting thing? She was not sure what she wept for more. His friendship or the passion they had discovered together.

Suffice it to say, she may have poured more emotion into their first correspondence than intended, but she meant every word. She might be starting out on her own, but she knew deep down she would have never found the courage had it not been for Jacob. Never found who she hoped to become if he had not helped free her from the cage of her last marriage. Yet he *had* freed her, and that became clearer by the day. The very hour. She chose not to read his letter right away but saved it for her journey back to Scotland when it came.

First, however, she must tackle her journey south.

"Are you quite sure you want to do this?" Maude asked one last time as she stood with Prudence outside her carriage less than a week later. She looked at her with curiosity. With the hint of a proud smile. "Because you could just as easily head north and never look back."

"I could," she granted. "But I get the sense the best way to let go of my past is to face it rather than run from it." She shrugged. "Even if it is nothing but brick and stucco now."

"Wise words, my sister." Maude embraced her, the smile in her voice obvious. "I very much look forward to visiting you in your new home once you are settled."

"And I look forward to having you." Prudence held Maude at arm's length and spoke from the heart. Meant every word. "Thank you, sister." She bit back emotion. "For everything."

"No need to thank me." Maude embraced her again. "It was such a pleasure seeing you again. I have missed you so very much." She looked at her again. "*This* you."

She had missed *this* her as well and was so glad she had found herself again. Where Agnus would have offered a stiff nod hello on the way here weeks ago, the small smile she offered Prudence now when she climbed into her carriage said much about their stay.

More so about the friendship they were discovering.

"This has been quite the time, has it not, Miss Agnus?" The carriage pulled away, and she silently bid farewell to a castle that had been at the root of so much. She glanced up at the battlements and whispered farewell to Jacob in her mind. Would never forget the time they had spent up there, most especially.

"It has, my lady." Agnus glanced out the window as well. "Who knew the Scottish would be so amiable?"

"Were they all, then?" That had sounded rather nostalgic. She sat back and perked a brow at Agnus, comfortable being frank with her. "Did you make peace with the duke's valet at the end?"

"As I have said time and time again, there was no peace to be made." Agnus' huffy response gave her away. "I can say, however, I appreciated his discreetness when we exchanged letters on your and the duke's behalf."

While she suspected there was more to it than that, she rather liked watching her maid soften along with her. Or should she say, become a little less strict in her way of thinking? Either way, they had shared more words at MacLauchlin Castle than they had during all their years in Mayfair. They had even talked of Agnus' family when she styled Prudence's hair. Her life before joining her. And she had enjoyed it more than she thought she might; she rather liked Agnus and suspected her maid felt the same about her.

A fact proven when Agnus agreed to move to Scotland with her.

To that end, she was grateful to have her maid with her when they eventually pulled up in front of her Mayfair home. Grateful to have a friend by her side when the carriage doors swung open, and she peered up at the window she had gazed through weeks before.

Looked up at what had felt so much like a prison.

"Are you ready, then, my lady?" Agnus said, not gently but firmly. She jutted out her chin and looked from Prudence to their former home. "For I will be by your side every step of the way."

"I am," she said without hesitation and squared her shoulders, ready to go to war with her past. "More than you could possibly know."

# Chapter Twelve

OUTSIDE OF LOSING his late wife, nothing was harder for Jacob than saying goodbye to Prudence. Watching her fade into the distance as his carriage made its way over the MacLauchlin's drawbridge. How very beautiful she had looked. Poignant in her stance when he knew this was not easy for either of them.

While determined to wait until he was home and alone before reading her letter, he found himself breaking the seal before they even reached the gates. Before she was gone from his sight, and he did not see her again for God knows how long.

He could not help but smile at how she had addressed him.

*23 November 1815*

*My Dearest Jacob,*

*I thought to write you a formal letter of thanks for all you have shown and taught me over the past week but feel that pales in comparison to what you just showed me on the battlements. How I felt in your arms when you looked at me. Kissed me.*

*Truth be told, I never meant for things to go so far so fast. Therefore, I feel I must apologize. For what, you ask? All of it and none of it, I suppose. For looking forward to every moment I spent with you while, at the same time, knowing it was not what I could give you in the end. Not if I ever hoped to find myself once more.*

*Or a version of myself, I should say.*

*I wish things had been different. That I had been a different woman when you met me. That I was worldly and wise and able to throw caution to the wind with your proposal. More than that, though, that I did not need to rediscover myself first. But I did, and still do. Fortunately, you understood that and let me go when I know you wanted to hold onto me as tightly as I did you.*

*So once more, my deepest thanks, Your Grace. Jacob. My dearest friend.*

*Until we meet again,*
*Prudence*

"Are you quite all right, Your Grace?" Donal asked.

He blinked and looked at his valet sitting across from him. "Aye. Why do you ask?"

"I suppose because of your expression," he said, having been asked to be honest years ago. "You seem distressed."

"Perhaps because I am." He stared out the window. "When I have no right to be, my friend."

"I see."

Hearing the tightness in Donal's voice, he glanced his way. "I take it you disapprove?"

"I do not, Your Grace." He gestured at the letter. "Rather, as much as it pains me to see such an expression on your face, I cannot help but welcome it."

He arched his eyebrows. "I dare say?"

"It seems I dare say as well, Your Grace." Donal's gaze flickered from the letter back to Jacob, his forthrightness to such a degree, rare. "You have found a happiness with Lady Barrington you have not felt in years, have you not?"

"I have," he admitted without a second thought. Without nary a hesitation.

"Then perhaps you should not be so crestfallen when reading her letter?" Donal's usually staunch demeanor softened. "Rather, mayhap you should look forward to the future, no matter how long it may take in coming?"

He did not want to wait, and Donal saw that clearly enough. Although tempted to say such and rail against not following Prudence from Mayfair to Dalness straight away, he knew better and understood that this leg of the journey was for her and her alone.

That did not mean he would not be with her every step of the way via letters, though. To that end, he wrote her back en route and had the letter delivered when they stopped halfway home. Had it sent directly to Mayfair so she might receive it upon her arrival. His words were not ones of affection, per se, but a brief note of support. Strength he knew she could use. Words that might bring a smile to her face when such was needed.

And it was the first of many letters he wrote her daily, even if he did not send them all.

*24 November 1815*

*My Dearest Prudence,*

*I can only hope you arrived safely at Mayfair and that you stormed the front gates of your enemy's castle. That you laid siege and took no prisoners. For I can see you in all your glory, chin held high, shoulders thrust back, as you breached their defenses.*

*Know that I stand by you in spirit always, every inch your second-in-command. I hope you saw your way free of all that stood in your way and laid waste to all those demons. Ever the conqueror. That in the end, you came out the victor, as I am quite sure you did.*

*Until next time, fair warrior.*

*Your Stalwart Protector,*
*Jacob*

After that, their banter and growing friendship only flour-ished. While there were a few longer, more heartfelt letters in between that made things harder than they already were, they largely kept things brief and took on the role of a lord and lady from yesteryear. It became an entertaining bond that kept a smile on their faces when he imagined every moment apart was as hard on her as it was him.

*15 December 1815*

*My Dearest Second-in-Command,*

*I am pleased to report I laid siege to the castle knowing you stood by me every step of the way. It was not an easy fight at first, mainly because my own pesky soldiers disguised as memories got in the way, but when everything was said and done, all bowed before me.*

*Moreover, I am pleased to report that he who stood watch at the gate has opted to journey forth to my new home in Scotland with me. You remember me telling you about the fellow. A certain butler, Mr. Fenwick, who lumbered with teeth bared at the door? Or better put, with beady eyes as he scowled so much one could not see his teeth.*

*Nonetheless, after many a day of evil eyes and beastly looks down his pointy chin, he finally succumbed and decided he would protect his new queen when thrust into the wilds of an unkempt country. So having turned my castle over to another, I now journey forth to my much more impressive estate north of the border.*

*Your Appreciative Commander,*
*Prudence*

Jacob chuckled and grinned at Donal as he helped him put on his suit jacket. "Are we Scots so unkempt then, my friend?"

"Indeed not, Your Grace." Donal looked down his nose every bit as much as Jacob imagined her butler did. "If anything, we are verra much the opposite."

Jacob meant to reiterate that in a letter, too, but things became busy. Non-stop until the holiday was upon him, and he longed for her more than ever. Wondered what she might look like in a Christmastide gown. He fantasized endlessly about how she had looked in that blue gown when last he saw her.

Many a night and too many mornings to count, he remembered the warmth of her lips beneath his. How sweet she tasted. How lost he had become in a mere kiss. Lost in a way he had not been since his late wife.

Perhaps, however hard to believe, more lost.

The way Prudence responded to him on the MacLauchlin's battlements had been intoxicating. He had not thought she would let things go that far. That she would have allowed him to touch her like that. Feel her sweet heat. Bring her to her peak.

Watching her head fall back, eyes slide shut, and her lips part as she struggled to draw in air, had been intoxicating. The bliss on her face had aroused him to no end. Made him so hard he was shocked he did not take her then and there.

Because they had wanted it.

Needed it.

Yet he had held back and was thankful now. Grateful he had not yanked up her dress and thrust deep inside her. Because if he had, he might have never let her go. Never let her out of his sight again for the sake of knowing he would need her again too soon. That no other would measure up. Could not.

Having Prudence like that would be his end in a way he did not quite understand yet. Feeling her from the inside out. Because it would be just that. A merging of flesh and soul he knew he could never turn from.

So they wrote.

*25 December 1815*

*My Beloved Commander,*

*I hope you have since journeyed forth to your new kingdom and found the wonderful new beginning you have long sought. Oh, but to see you flourish in such a place, surrounded by those who would not think to oppress you.*

*To see you stand tall on your own battlements.*

*I wish you a lovely holiday and wish more than ever I was there to see you settle in and find your own way. Watch as you make a castle your own for the first time. Be by your side as you soften your stance but keep your weapons at the ready lest any enemy slip past your defenses.*

*Your Dearest Second-in-Command,*
*Jacob*

He was quite sure she had not let anyone mar her new life. Would not. His speculation was confirmed when Emma and her husband visited. While he wanted to ask how Prudence fared the moment they arrived at his home, he knew better. First, they had to get through the pomp and fuss of a holiday that seemed duller than ever without Prudence in it.

Eventually, he and Emma strolled arm and arm alone, and he finally asked what he longed to know. Waited with bated breath for her answer.

"How is Prudence…truly?"

"She is well, my friend." She smiled. "Really well."

When she looked at him with reassurance, he felt like a weight lifted from his shoulders. It was one thing for Prudence to banter and claim such in a letter. Another thing altogether to hear proof of it.

"She has sold her late husband's estate and moved into her new home in Dalness." Heartfelt fondness lit her eyes. "You should have seen her. She was—"

"So you saw?" He interrupted her because he could not help himself. "You were there with her?"

"I was, given she purchased one of my manors, and I wanted to show her around." Emma's smile only warmed as she went on. "I feared she might be disappointed having purchased it sight unseen, but she seemed quite the opposite."

"Tell me," he said softly, again wishing he had been there. "Tell me everything. Spare no detail."

So Emma did, and he could see it all because he had been

there before. From the way Prudence's jaw dropped at the sizeable house surrounded by trees to the mountains looming proudly behind it.

"It is hard to describe her response other than to say she was in awe from start to finish," Emma said. "She touched everything tentatively as though she could hardly believe it was hers." He heard the emotion in her voice. "Considering the outstanding house she came from, I am not sure I have ever seen anyone admire an estate, really more of an upscale country manor, like she did her new home. It might as well have been Buckingham Palace or Edinburgh Castle."

"Without doubt," he murmured, seeing Prudence there as though he stood beside her. As if he sensed the wonder and freedom she had surely felt. "What did she do first?"

"Funny you would ask."

"Why?"

"Because I swore I heard her whisper, wonder, what you would have her do first."

"Surely not."

"Perhaps not, but I swore...."

When she trailed off, he frowned. "So what did she do?" he prompted. "How did she imagine I might respond?"

"Do you really want to know?" She narrowed an eye at him. "Because it was quite strange."

"Of course I do." His heart leapt. "I would not have asked otherwise."

"Well, she was curious if there was any sort of look-out point, so to speak." She considered him like he might know what that was about. "A battlement of sorts on a country house. Can you even imagine?"

"I can." He cleared his throat. "I very much can."

"Somehow, I suspected you might answer that way." Emma cast him a sly look. "So, fortunately, I was able to answer that aye, indeed there was."

He frowned. "But there is not."

"Perhaps when last you visited." She shrugged her shoulder. "But things do change, and new outlooks, even from a rhetorical battlement on top of a manor, can be created in very little time. More of a widow's watch, as Americans might call it."

"Dear lord, woman," he exclaimed. Did she know what had happened that night on MacLauchlin Castle's battlements? He should have protected Prudence from such scandal and never done it in the first place.

"No need to fear, my friend." Emma rested a hand on his arm and looked at him most seriously. "No one knows of your little tryst with Lady Barrington, not even I to its extent, for Maude and I made sure your tracks were well-covered."

"Which means at least one knew," he concluded. "One who ensured all stayed away lest anyone come upon us?"

"Though quieter, it was the end of a holiday, and people *were* still about the castle," she reminded. "But that is neither here nor there. What matters is what came of it, and that was beautiful, aye?"

"Undeniably," he said softly, wishing he were back there this very moment.

"Good then," Emma said just as softly. "So is a much scaled-down battlement on a Scottish country manor. Which is not all bad if it helps put the same look on her face that you wear now, I would say."

While unsure what such a structure would look like, he appreciated the gesture and said as much. He then kept Prudence with him for the remainder of the night via Emma's memories, yet nothing was quite like hearing from her.

So he read her next letter and could not stop himself from smiling yet again.

*3 January 1816*

*My Loving Second-in-Command,*

*I must say I am most taken by my new castle and its subjects. Some old and some new, but all quite loyal. Even the former monster at the gate. Be sure to brace yourself for I have impact-ful news. That monster even went so far as to offer the hint of a smile the other day.*

*Yes, you read that correctly. My stalwart English butler de-fied the rules of his late and very unlawful king and indulged in the upturn of the corner of his lips. It was brief, most certainly fleeting, but it has given us all great hope that the dragon guarding our gates might be more welcoming to strangers going forward.*

*As to other things. The holidays were lovely, but I must admit they would have been better enjoyed with my second-in-command by my side. I hope you fare well and look forward to hearing from you soon.*

*Your Beloved and Lonely Commander,*
*Prudence*


He stared at the word 'lonely' for some time. Wanted to rush to her immediately but knew better. She was finding her way and saying what made sense. Besides, he could not go to her if he wanted to. He had too much business in which to attend. Things his new position made impossible to avoid. While he considered sending her jewelry, he suspected she would frown upon it. That it might make her feel like a kept woman when she was no such thing.

So he wrote, hoping his words told her everything she needed to know.

Everything he had come to feel.

*15 January 1816*

*My Much Missed and Beloved Commander,*

*I would be by your side if I could. Defend you 'til my last dying breath. Unfortunately, the weight of a kingdom weighs heavily on me, and I must see to my people. Might you travel the land and visit me? For I would pay a ransoms weight in gold to see you.*

He paused with his quill over the paper, debating how blunt he should be but decided there was no other way. Not when it came to Prudence and how much he missed her.

*Moreover, I would pay anything to hold you again, my commander. Kiss you. Taste you...*

Know you were mine. Love you in ways you have never been loved before. Keep you safe until the end of time. All words, of course, he did not pen yet but felt more by the moment. Hour. Week. Month.

*Your Devoted and Equally Lonely Second-in-Command,*
*Jacob*

Despite endless business, it felt like the days ticked by far too slowly as he awaited her response. One that took longer than usual. So long he dreaded it when it came. Feared it, that is, until he opened it and knew whether he was Duke of Argyll or not, he had no choice but to obey.

*19 February 1816*

*Dear Second-in-Command,*

*I demand you come pay respects to your liege.*

*Awaiting Your Arrival,*
*Prudence*

# Chapter Thirteen

P RUDENCE PEERED OUT over the snowy Scottish woodland and flinched. Should she have sent that last message to Jacob? It was one thing to banter flirtatiously. Another thing altogether to make such a demand of the Duke of Argyll.

Because when all was said and done, he was an important man with a lot of responsibilities, and she but a widow. Prudence lowered her hood despite the heavy snowfall and breathed in the icy air. Relished the cool wind and smiled at Agnus before she closed her eyes and tilted her face up to catch the plump, dancing snowflakes.

She might be a widow, but she was happy.

Most days, she was so happy she thought she might burst from the feel of it. Moving to Dalness had been the best decision of her life. From the moment she spied her new home through the sweeping trees, she had been in love. If ever a spot could be considered magical, she had found it. From the thick, lush forests she could not wait to see bloom in springtime to the towering mountains and sweeping glens she simply stared at for hours.

Her trip back to Mayfair had been more freeing than antici-pated, and surprisingly enough, the remaining staff had wanted to stay with her, including her butler, Mr. Fenwick. She could not fathom why until Agnus made it clear they had always liked her more than her late husband. And employment was employment.

Even if it meant leaving behind proper society and trudging into the wilds of Scotland to work alongside those hired locally.

Since then, those who braved this new life with her had settled in well. Which she was thankful for, given what Emma referred to as a "quaint country manor" was indeed sizeable and needed a staff. Not an overly large one, but enough to see to the kitchen, study, library, drawing room, dining room, twenty or so bedrooms, a carriage house, stables, and gardens.

Emma and Maude had visited several times since she moved in, recommending one vendor or another to see to new curtains and furnishings if she wished them. Emma had sold her the estate "as is," which turned out to be quite the bargain, given the furnishings that had been left behind. It was something Prudence had commented on, but her new friend had waved off.

"This is a fresh start, my dear," Emma had said. "Keep things or not. It is all yours."

Where she had thought Emma did it for Jacob, and she still very well might have, over time, Prudence began to believe it had more to do with her than him. Better still, that she truly liked Prudence and wanted this new start for her.

So here she stood on her battlement as she and Jacob had called it in their letters and wondered yet again if she should have demanded he come. Had she pushed their lively banter one step too far? Because somehow it felt less like banter over time and more like thinly veiled love letters.

At least all the ones she had not sent.

"You are writing him again, my lady?" Agnus had asked just the other night. "Might I send this one?"

"Yes," she said impulsively, staring down at her curt message. "No." She had glanced at Agnus and frowned. "I do not know."

"Then this one must make the cut." Agnus held out her hand, leaving no room for argument. "I will see it sent first thing in the morning."

Like all before it, Prudence sealed it with wax and her crest, so it was ready to go. Was she ready to send it, though?

"My lady." Agnus' brows shot up, and she held her hand out more firmly. "Your letter?"

Not about to get on her maid's bad side when her good side was proving so very enjoyable, she handed the letter over and prayed for a miracle. She hoped Jacob would not take one look at it after all this time and toss it into the flames of the nearest fire.

Granted, it had not been overly long between letters but longer than usual, and it was all her fault. Not because she was busy or distracted but because every letter she wrote suddenly seemed too intimate. Felt too desperate. How could they not when she missed him so much? When, despite her wonderful new life, she still thought about him daily? Wished she could share every little bit of her adventure with him without feeling like it was over the top? Feeling like he probably had more important things in which to attend?

"My lady?"

"Yes, Miss Agnus?" Her eyes were still closed, and her face upturned to the sky.

"You must attend your company."

"Must I?" she said absently, so lost in thought it did not occur to her no one should be visiting given the snowy weather.

"My lady." Agnus sounded quite insistent. "You must attend who comes."

She opened her eyes to the elegant carriage pulling down the drive. One as obsidian and sharp as its owner's eyes.

"Miss Agnus." She clutched her friend's arm. "Is that what I think it is? *Who* I think it is?"

"If you think it might be the Duke of Argyll, my lady," Agnus' eyes brightened, "I would say that is a safe assumption."

"Good God, he listened to my summons?"

Agnus bit back a smile. "If that was in the last missive you allowed me to send, then it certainly seems so."

Never so excited, she flew downstairs only to stop short at the door when her butler blocked the way. His finely plucked eyebrows furrowed. "My lady."

She frowned. "Yes, Mr. Fenwick?"

"Whatever are you doing?" His mouth flattened into an uncompromising line. "For surely a lady of your stature does not intend to rush out this door when royalty approaches."

"Actually, I did." And she would have.

His brows lowered sharply. "Yet you will not."

Some might say he spoke out of turn, given he was under her employ and she a lady, but she had come to realize Fenwick was on a quest. Or so Agnus had claimed. It seemed, despite his stalwart, haughty manner, he really was quite fond of Prudence and would see her keep her manners despite where they had moved.

Despite how remarkable the change in her.

"I should like to go outside and greet the duke," she repeated. "So please let me by, Mr. Fenwick."

"Not quite yet." Agnus nodded at Fenwick that he had done well stopping her and started barking orders at the staff to revive the hearths and ready food. Then, with the precision of the soldier Prudence knew she could be, Agnus busied herself with Prudence's appearance.

"If you intend to run down icy stairs, which I highly discourage," Agnus muttered, "then it will be in more sturdy and fashionable boots than what you currently wear, my lady."

Prudence thanked Fenwick for his supportive arm as Agnus, foot by foot, yanked off her shoes and replaced them with something more appropriate.

"Very good, then," Prudence said once properly attired. Ready to race outside, she grinned at Fenwick, only for him to frown and shake his head. Agnus shot him another thankful look as she brushed lingering snow off of Prudence and smoothed her hair. To top off the look both seemed to be striving for, Agnus pulled one of her finer fur-lined coats out of what seemed like thin air and helped her into it.

So impatient she could scream, she glanced from her maid to her butler as they eyed her over. "Do I meet your approval now?"

"Yes, I do believe—"

"Good." Making her way past them, she rushed out the door and flew down the stairs, only for them to follow. She bit back a sigh and looked back and forth between them when they fell in step beside her. "What now? I thought all was well."

"And it is," Fenwick granted.

"As long as you remember where this all began with the Lord of Argyll, my lady," Agnus finished for him as Jacob's coach pulled up. "And it was not with you acting as anything less than a lady."

"Because you *are* a lady," Fenwick reminded. "Might you never forget it."

Where she had intended to bypass Jacob's footman and make her way into his carriage, much like Maude had when Prudence first arrived at MacLauchlin Castle, she realized they were right.

She was acting impulsively.

Inappropriately.

So she ignored her racing heart and folded her hands neatly in front of her when the carriage stopped. When Jacob stepped out, and their gazes connected for the first time in what felt like ages, her breath caught.

Just like that, everything faded away, and all she could see was him. She knew Fenwick and Agnus curtsied and bowed. Knew they said, "Welcome, Your Grace," but it all seemed to come from a great distance away. As though she and Jacob were alone all over again on the MacLauchlin Castle battlements, and the pleasantries around them but an echo on the wind.

"My dear Lady Barrington." Jacob kissed her gloved hand, his gaze lingering on her face. "I cannot tell you how good it is to see you again."

Finally finding her tongue and good manners, she curtsied, her voice a bit hoarse even to her own ears. "Welcome, Your Grace. I did not expect your arrival." She glanced from the darkening sky to him. "Especially with such inclement weather arriving soon."

The corner of his mouth inched up. His tone turned teasing, and a twinkle lit his eyes. "Was I not summoned then, my liege?"

She might have let Fenwick and Agnus take the reins of good propriety up until now, but she was no longer the sort who avoided banter. So she certainly would not with Jacob.

Not when they had such fun together.

"You certainly were summoned, dear second-in-command." An all-too-familiar warmth curled through her as his gaze continued lingering on her face with unmistakable affection. "And I must say, you did so in remarkably good time."

"But of course, my lady, though you did not need to meet me at my carriage in such weather." He held out his elbow. "May I escort you back inside?"

"You may." Her heart continued racing, and her skin grew warmer still as she slipped her arm into his. She had missed the feel of him so very much. Too much. And she said so in a roundabout way. "I cannot tell you how happy I am to see you again, Your Grace. Truly very happy."

"I could not agree more, my lady." He steered her closer to him as they climbed the stairs. His voice lowered lest he be overhead. "More than you can possibly imagine."

Her throat thickened with emotion at the longing in his voice. A longing that mirrored what she had felt every moment they were apart.

"May I offer you a refreshment, Your Grace?" she said when they stepped inside, and Fenwick took their coats. "You must be weary after such a long journey."

"I would like that," he said. "Whisky if you have it."

"Of course." She had made sure it was in stock lest he visit. "Let us warm ourselves by the fire and catch up."

"You will find whisky and food awaiting you in the study, Your Grace." Agnus nodded once at her. "My lady."

"Thank you, Miss Agnus." Leave it to her maid to have anticipated precisely what Jacob would want. "You are efficient as always."

"Indeed you are, Miss Agnus," Jacob praised. Prudence did not miss the well-disguised glimmer of amusement in his eyes. "As I am sure Mr. Fenwick has much to see to, would you mind familiarizing my valet, Mr. Donal, with the servants' quarters? I believe you two became acquainted at MacLauchlin Castle?"

"We did, Your Grace." Agnus did not bat a lash. "A very amiable fellow, if I recall."

"Very much so." Jacob played right along. "I do believe he thought you quite amiable as well, Miss Agnus."

"Will you be staying overnight then, Your Grace?" Prudence asked, surprised. It felt as though butterflies flittered around in her stomach. *Please say yes. Never leave if you can manage it.*

"I was rather hoping so with the incoming storm." He looked from her servants to her. "If it would not put everyone out too much?"

"Not at all," she said. "We have more than enough room." She knew it to be bold but could care less when she addressed Agnus. "As it is one of the warmest when the wind comes in from the north, please see the room beside mine readied for the duke."

Well aware of how inappropriate some might think the location, Fenwick stiffened. "Are you quite sure, my lady? There is always the room—"

"Quite sure, Mr. Fenwick." She looked from her maid to her butler. "Now, if you two would see to your duties, the duke and I do not wish to be disturbed while we catch up."

Before either could say a word, she escorted Jacob into the study only to find herself swept into his arms the moment the door clicked shut.

"You cannot know what you have done to me, Prudence," he said softly, cupping her cheek. "Cannot know how badly I have missed you."

She had no chance to reply before his mouth closed over hers, and they were right back on that battlement. Right back in a moment, she had fantasized about more times than she could count.

Kissing him.

Loving him.

Because that had to be what this was, or something very much akin.

What else could it be when she once again floated? Once more lost herself in him? Some might say it mere lust, but it felt like more. As if it possessed something beyond just matters of the flesh. Yet matters of the flesh were certainly there when he pulled her more firmly against him, and she felt his arousal. Just like before, the ache between her thighs only intensified.

Their kisses turned more passionate until he groaned and rested his forehead against hers. "I fear if I keep kissing you, I will not be able to stop." His voice sounded guttural. Desperate. "And this study is no better a place to have you than a battlement would have been."

"I tend to disagree." Her voice was equally strained. "I think the battlements would have been most daring."

"Are you such a daring sort then, my lady?" He smiled and pulled back just enough to see her undoubtedly flushed face. The sparkle in her eyes. "Ah, but then it seems you very much are, nowadays." He caressed her cheek. "And while I applaud that, you deserve better." As though he had trouble finding his voice once again, his words dropped to an emotional whisper. "So much better."

"And what do you consider better?" Because, quite frankly, it would not matter where they were. She was aware of only him when in his arms.

"I will know it when I see it." He led her to the sofa in front of the fire. "Until then, simply being near you will have to do."

"And so you are." She sat and smiled, then nodded yes to a glass of claret when he went to prepare them both a drink. "I cannot believe you came. That you are actually here."

"You say that as though you feared I might never." He sat pleasantly close after giving her the glass of claret. "Surely you knew I would come? That there is nowhere else I would rather be?"

She had hoped but dared not say it lest she seem too obvious.

"I am in complete agreement." She could not help but keep smiling because he was every bit as much a part of her newfound happiness as this house. "Tell me everything you did not say in your letters, Jacob, for we got in a pattern of being brief, did we not?"

"We did." He grinned. "But what fun it was."

She met his grin. "Indeed." Even so, she wanted to hear it all, if for no other reason than to listen to his voice. "Yet still, life has been busy for us both, so do let us catch up as we claimed we would."

And so they did, falling into the easy comradery they had enjoyed from nearly the beginning. He went into details about the latest happenings at his estate, and she, of course, shared everything about her travels back to Mayfair, then her return adventure into Scotland.

"It is clear Dalness, and the fresh Scottish air agrees with you," Jacob said at one point. "You look more beautiful than ever, Prudence." He trailed the pad of his thumb along her jawline. "Truly radiant."

"I do love it here." She nearly closed her eyes to his touch. "The people are just as kind as they were at MacLauchlin Castle. While smaller, my local village is equally charming. Then there is the countryside." Anticipation filled her. "I long to see it during every season. To stroll through its forests and perhaps try fishing in its waters."

"Fishing." His eyebrows flew up. "Truly?"

"Yes." She cocked her head. "Does that surprise you?"

"If I were to compare it to the rather uppity lass I first chatted with on a sofa much like this in MacLauchlin Castle, I would say very much so." He rested his elbow on the back of the sofa and played with a tendril of her hair that had come loose. "Now?" His finger dusted the side of her neck as though he could not help but touch her. "Now, I believe fishing is the very least of what you might be capable of." His eyes grew hopeful. "Might I teach you when the time comes?"

"I would like that very much." She looked at him curiously. "Though I must admit, I am surprised to learn you fish."

"Why, when I grew up on the water?"

"I suppose you did," she said. "But I know little more than that about you and find I would like to learn more. We have talked about many things but not those that matter most."

"Quite right."

When his smile faded and he did not go on, she could not help but reflect on what Emma had told her about him finding much-needed happiness with his late wife. How it implied life had not been so kind before that. She rested her hand on his arm. "Only if you want to, Jacob. Speaking of your past is not a prerequisite to our friendship."

"But perhaps it should be," he said softly, his gaze most serious. "Because we both know this is much more than mere friendship."

"Yet not quite courtship," she clarified, making sure he understood. "As I said when last we met, I do not desire marriage again." She shivered at the thought. "I will not suffer that again."

"Then perhaps we start there in our not-quite courtship." He rested his hand over hers. "Tell me more about your marriage, Prudence. More so, what you were like before it."

"Before it, I was…." What, exactly? "I think precisely as I am now, only more naïve." While she would much rather never have spared another thought about her late husband, let alone speak of him, she found the words tumbling out of her mouth regardless. "As implied in the ballroom before you and I first danced, my husband, Randolph, was anything but faithful. I would like to say he managed fidelity during the first few months of our marriage, but somehow, I doubt it."

She paused a moment, thinking about it.

"As to who I was coming into my marriage?" She shook her head, wondering how she had drifted so far from her ideals. "I suppose I hoped my elevation in society would help me procure change. That I could show others those in the upper crest were no better than the working class." She sighed, ashamed of herself. "Yet, I suspect I did the opposite. Moreover, I became capable of what I did to you, and for that, I will forever be sorry."

"I have made it clear that part of our lives is behind us, and I meant it." Jacob wrapped his fingers with hers. "As to what you became, might it not be looked at as a learning experience rather than something you regret?" He shook his head. "You are not that lass anymore, Prudence. You are anything but, and I believe, an even better person for it. Just watching Agnus and your butler fawn over you proves that. You mean a great deal to your servants."

"Were they fawning?" She quirked the corner of her mouth. "Because it felt a tad more like suffocating. Or at least it did before you arrived."

"Even so, it is clear they only want the best for you." He winked. "So says their concern over your good name when it comes to a second-in-command raiding your castle and blockading you in here so I might ravish you at will."

"Did you do all that, then?" She chuckled. "Because it felt rather like your liege gave you little choice."

"A good ruler, indeed." He pressed his lips to the back of her hand, his gaze very much aligned with his murmured words against her sensitive flesh. "Might she conquer me at will."

"She might very well," she said so softly it might as well have been a whisper. The truth was, she could think of nothing better. Wondered so very much what it might feel like.

To that end, she made herself especially clear.

# Chapter Fourteen

EVERY MINUTE OF every hour of the carriage ride had been pure torture. Every mile had been agonizing and drawn out especially knowing he would have to wait until day's end to lay eyes on Prudence once again. To pull her into his arms and kiss her soundly. Kiss her until she understood just how much he had come to care for her.

Now here she was saying something most forward yet highly anticipated.

"You should know I have educated myself on ways to prevent things from happening that should not out of wedlock," she said softly. "If we are to embark on a not-quite-courtship relationship, then we should do so responsibly."

While Jacob might argue there was risk regardless, he sensed she need not be told. Instead, he found himself put off in a way he had no right to be. She was not his. They were not married. Yet something about the idea of her not wanting to have a child with him seemed wrong. As though he were the only one with whom she should ever want to share such a gift.

"You seem disappointed." Her eyebrows edged together slowly. "Perhaps I misunderstood where this might be heading?"

"You did not." He wanted to be between her thighs so badly it hurt. "I appreciate your vigilance, Prudence. I only wish it were not the case."

He could tell by her continued confusion, she understood no more than he did what he alluded to. Not really. Rather than say it because it would only be a marriage proposal she did not want, he sidestepped somewhat and walked himself into a difficult subject he would have preferred avoiding.

"What I mean to say is I am not so sure I can have wee bairns." However painful, he continued because she deserved to know. "Elizabeth and I tried for years to no avail."

"I am so sorry." Prudence squeezed his hand. The look in her eyes reflected his sadness. "Unfortunately, I can relate as I am fairly certain I am incapable of having children, too. Even so…"

"Even so," he echoed, wondering at her tension. "What is it?" He searched her eyes, concerned by her pain. "Were you that eager then, despite how unfortunate your marriage?"

"Very much so." She sighed. "Or at least, at first, when I thought our child would come into a loving home. After that, it became an endless duty at which I forever failed. Then, eventually, it was a dreaded duty I prayed I failed at."

If her blasted late husband was in front of him now, he would call him out for putting her through so much misery. For not cherishing her like she deserved to be cherished.

"You did not fail him." He nearly called her his love but stopped himself. "Rather, it was the opposite. Might you never forget it."

"Did you know him then?"

"I knew *of* him," he confessed. "And I can promise you this, Prudence. Any fault in your marriage, or who you became over the years, was solely because of him and no one else." He tilted her chin until she had no choice but to look at him. "It is important that you know that. More so, it is important that you forgive yourself for the woman you became during those difficult years."

"I know," she murmured. "And I usually do."

"Yet it needs to be *always*." He could not help but brush his lips across hers. Taste her sweetness again, however briefly. "All that is behind you now. You are a free and very desired lass. One, as you said, who has found her way back to being a better person."

"No small thanks to you." Prudence rubbed her lips together as if holding onto his taste as well. "I cannot tell you how much I have come to value our friendship, Jacob."

"And I yours." So much so when tempted to kiss her again, he held back and gave her more than intended. So much so when tempted to kiss her again, he refrained lest he lose himself to the kiss and not tell her things he wanted her to know. Things he had never shared with anyone but Elizabeth. "To that end, I will share my past with you, however much I detest it."

He went on to tell her what it had been like to be raised as the inheriting son of an earl in the Rothesay household. Or, as it were, their adjoining home, as it was uncouth for his parents to have their bairns about overly much. He told her how he'd never quite measured up. Never enjoyed love or adoration from either parent.

"And it made me into a beastly, angry young man." He looked at the fire rather than see even a glimmer of disappointment in Prudence's eyes. "I was uncaring to lasses. Cruel, even. Pompous, because I had no idea how else to be. Thrust into a life of wealth and privilege I had not earned. To which I felt entitled. I was above myself in every way possible and let all those around me know it." He shook his head and tried not to stare too deeply into the past. "Meeting Elizabeth was nothing shy of a miracle. She saved me in ways I cannot tell you. Made me a better person."

"And you *are* a better person, Jacob." Prudence cupped his cheek and steered his gaze back to her face. To what seemed loving eyes. "One who went on to save me just as much as Elizabeth saved you. I might not have known her, but I cannot help but think Elizabeth would have liked that. She seems the sort who would have."

"She was," he said. "Very much so."

Guilt flared at the assumption she had been the first lass he tried to save. He should tell her now she was not the first but struggled to tell her. Feared how she might react. Even worse, he realized how terrified he was that she might turn him away if she discovered the truth. Nevertheless, he needed to tell her and was about to when she set aside their drinks, cupped his cheeks, and kissed him. Kissed him so passionately that his good intentions vanished, and he pulled her onto his lap.

After that, all he could do was kiss her. Lose himself in what would normally be a simple act but seemed so much more with her. She wore a different scent than she had at the beginning, and he relished the soft, feminine aroma. Wanted more of it. *Her.* So when she steered his hand to her breast, he could not help but caress the soft mound. Dust his fingers over her nipple when it pebbled. Wanted her so much when she pulled up her dress and straddled him, he allowed it rather than fought it.

"This is not where," he began, but she took the words out of his mouth when she kissed him again. When their tongues twirled and twisted, he drowned in her.

Lost himself in a place where good intentions became a distant memory.

Instead, he groaned as their kisses grew hungrier, and she rubbed her warm center against him. Desperate for her, he clenched the firm globes of her backside and steered her back and forth over his clothed erection until he swore he would burst.

"Jacob," she moaned, clearly unwilling to stop. She yanked at the strings of his trousers. "Please."

"Are you sure," he managed, so aroused it hurt. "Are you—"

Prudence put a finger to his lips and looked at him with so much desire, there could be no mistaking she knew exactly what she wanted. Exactly what she was doing.

"I have never been surer of anything." Her cheeks were flushed with desire, and her breathing uneven as she moved her hips slowly. Enough to make him want to roar like a beast and slam into her until he slaked his lust. "So now I suppose the question is, are you?"

Their gazes held for a long, excruciating moment before he said all he was able.

"Since the moment I pulled you onto the dance floor." They never lost eye contact as he freed himself. Never looked away from one another as he slowly steered her onto his throbbing shaft. Her eyes drifted, and her breathing grew choppy. He clenched her backside again and groaned at the exquisite sensation of filling her hot, tight sheath.

Prudence braced her hands on his shoulders and sank down slowly. Like him, she seemed to relish every minuscule movement. Wanted to cherish and chase it all at once. Her mouth fell open, her eyes slid shut, and her head fell back when she fully seated herself.

"This is…" she whispered, her voice as choppy as her breathing. When she opened her eyes again, they were glassy with emotion. "You are…"

He gave her no chance to go on when he wrapped his hand around the back of her slender neck, pulled her against him, and kissed her. Not hard like he wanted to, but gently. With heart. All he felt which was more substantial than she might imagine.

Unending.

He hoped she felt as much when he let her remain in control. Let her do something he suspected had never even occurred to her late husband. Why would it when Prudence was vibrant and sensual, and Barrington was nothing of the sort? So even though Jacob touched her, loved her with his hands and eyes, he did nothing more than encourage her to take what she needed from him.

And she did.

She rolled her hips at first and made love to his arousal. Soon enough, however, she grew more confident and slid up and down his shaft so slowly it took almost more than he was capable of not to let go. Give in to the pressure building inside him. The incredible need to fill her with his seed.

To see her lose herself in climax like she had on the battlements.

This moment was for her, though. Hers to discover what it could be like with a man. Not one who pleasured her with his hand but his erection. With passion and a desire to see her satisfied before himself. Something he imagined her late husband had never afforded her.

Prudence's cheekbones flamed pink. Delicate beads of sweat pearled on her porcelain skin. She bit her lower lip as she drew closer. When a guttural groan began in her chest, he pulled her against him so she could bury her voice if need be. Then, he thrust up at the same pace she had been riding him until she locked up against him and muffled a ragged cry against his neck.

He bit back a groan at the feel of her sheath clamping down hard, then the untouchable sensation when she trembled in his arms and milked him. While not letting go might have been the hardest thing he had ever done, he stayed strong.

Gave her this.

Wanted it to be all about her.

When her breathing slowed at last, she pulled back and looked at him. Realized that he had not found fulfillment. Distressed, she drew her eyebrows together. "Was I...did I not please you?"

"You pleased me greatly, love," he said before he could stop himself. "But that was not about me." He brushed back the tendrils of hair slicked to her forehead. "That was about you. About finding your way back to the lass you were always supposed to be."

"Why does it sound like you were on a mission?" she murmured, skirting dangerously close to the truth. "As though you were never in this for yourself?"

"Because in some small way, I suppose I was not when we first crossed paths at MacLauchlin Castle." Closer still. "You deserve better than what your late husband gave you, Prudence. Better than what he made you become." He cupped her cheeks and searched her eyes. "Is it so wrong for me to want you to feel what you just felt? Find something I suspect you never did in your marriage?"

"No." Her eyes grew glassy again. "I just…" She swallowed hard and clearly decided against saying too much. Against making this moment about her late husband any more than need be. "Yet again, thank you, Jacob."

He went to respond but was unable to when she shifted, and his arousal leapt, by no means done with her. Clearly feeling as much, wanton in the womanly power she undoubtedly felt filling her, Prudence started rolling her hips again. He stopped breathing at the feel of her. The sight of her as she put her hands over his on her backside, slid up his shaft and stopped, making it clear he was in control now.

While tempted to give her time to bask in the afterglow of her orgasm, there was no man on earth who could refuse such an offering. Certainly not him. Therefore, despite his best intentions, he was helpless to do anything but steer her down then back up his arousal.

Thrust into her moist, welcoming heat.

Much to his delight, despite finding her own pleasure so recently, it seemed Lady Barrington very much enjoyed having matters taken out of her hands because she gasped, and her eyelashes fluttered. Lost in her response and how quickly she had become aroused again, he pulled her close once more and thrust harder. Deeper. Took all she offered.

Needed it like a dying man needed to breathe.

Yet drawing in air was impossible as blood rushed through him and drowned out all sound. Did away with anything but her tiny gasps of pleasure in his ear. Everything but her muffled cries as fire raced down his spine. His ballocks tightened so intensely he knew he was out of time. Knew it best he pulled out despite her assurances.

Regrettably, Prudence took the choice out of his hands when she gripped the back of the sofa and locked up so tightly against him, he was done for. He held onto her, buried a ragged groan in her soft hair, and exploded inside her.

Released in a way he never had before.

There was no other way to describe it. He felt euphoric. Gone in pure pleasure. Entrenched in losing himself at the precise moment she did. Needing to taste her, he pulled her lips to his and kissed her. Kissed her as she milked him once again, only making his pinnacle that much more intense. Kissed her until he knew if they did not stop, they would never leave this room. He would keep her prisoner until the end of time.

Until they made love at least a thousand more times.

So he eventually kissed her nose, then forehead before he pulled out, rested her cheek against his chest, and simply relished the feel of her in his arms. Cherished every precious moment. He smiled when her breathing slowed, and she drifted off to sleep. While tempted to wake her, he saw no reason. Rather, he pulled a throw blanket over her and rested his chin on the top of her head. Breathed in the flowery scent of her soft hair.

Had he ever felt like this before? Ever felt his heart swell in such a way after lovemaking? Surely he must have with Elizabeth. Not that their intimacy was quite like this. It had been beautiful. Special. But different somehow, and he was not sure why. Perhaps because the dynamics were so different? This time he was trying to bring Prudence back to who she should be where Elizabeth had been doing the same for him.

So was it all because he was saving Prudence, then? Was that half the thrill? He doubted it. If anything, it felt like she might be saving him. That in some strange way, this was the truest connection he'd ever had. Not just because of their undeniable chemistry but because of how similar they were. The friendship they had found. The incredible desire to be around each other. Talk until they could talk no more, which he suspected would be a day that never came.

Eventually, a light rap came at the door. "My lady, will you be dining?"

"Yes, Miss Agnus?" Prudence mumbled, stirring awake but clearly confused as to the time of day. "Just a few more minutes of sleep, then breakfast would be wonderful."

So he replied loud enough for Agnus to hear. "We will be dining, Miss Agnus. Thank you."

Prudence's head snapped up, and her sleepy gaze focused on his face. "Jacob."

"Prudence." He brushed her disarrayed hair away from her face and smiled. "I would say good morning, but it is still very much evening."

"Oh goodness." She blinked and took stock of her surroundings. Mainly that she still straddled him. "I am so sorry. I never meant to fall asleep on—"

He did not let her finish her sentence but cupped her cheeks and kissed her. Kissed her like he had wanted to since last they did mere hours ago.

"Never be sorry, love," he murmured against her lips. "Might you fall asleep time and time again after making me feel so good."

It seemed for all she enjoyed his kisses, using the word love yet again troubled her because she removed herself from his lap.

"Should you really voice such endearments?" She adjusted her clothing. "Is such not a bit much?"

While stung by her assessment, the last thing he intended to do was shy away from how he felt. "Not at all."

He stood and adjusted himself as well, then reeled her back into his arms before she headed for the door. Dug his hand into her hair gently until her gaze was forced to remain on his face. Forced to see the truth in his eyes.

Then he told her precisely what his endearment meant, whether she liked it or not.

# Chapter Fifteen

"IF YOU HAVE not figured it out by now, my fair lady and mighty liege," Jacob looked at Prudence in a way that made her toes curl and her heart go up in flames, "I call you my love because I have fallen in love with you."

Prudence tried to speak, but the words were trapped in her throat. Lodged in a brick of fear that was impossible to decipher other than she suspected it had everything to do with her late husband and nothing to do with Jacob. A sense of terror that had to do with him saying one thing now and possibly growling something hateful at her later.

Being a prince at the moment and a monster down the line.

"I am not him, Prudence." He caressed her cheek and saw inside her in a way no other could. "I am *me*. Jacob. Your friend, companion, lover, and in all ways that matter, very much your second-in-command and most devoted protector."

"But can you be all those things without wanting more?" she asked, when she finally found her voice. When she pushed past the way her foolish heart soared. When he voiced words that already reflected how strongly she felt too. "Because I cannot give you more, Jacob." She searched his eyes. Needed him to see the truth, however heartbreaking it may be. "I will not return to the prison of marriage. I refuse to put myself in another cage when I have so recently freed myself of the one before it."

Even if that cage was filled with lovemaking the likes of which she had never experienced. Even if she catapulted time and time again into that sort of bliss. Because it had very much been that. Jacob made her feel so incredibly good and immensely loved whether he realized it or not.

"I am not asking you to return to the prison of marriage." He shook his head. "I am just telling you what is in my heart, Prudence." There was no struggle in his voice or his expression as he continued. He meant what he said. "And I am telling you it is a love that will not go away whether we marry or not."

"Yet you must marry," she reminded, having had this drilled into her by Randolph time and time again. "Must produce an heir."

"I must do nothing of the sort, as my dukedom should have never been mine to begin with." He frowned. "I am not a Campbell by blood, so I do not owe them a legacy. I need never marry again and produce an heir if I do not wish to do so. Not to mention, as I already told you, I am fairly certain I could not if I tried."

"Would you if I said I wanted to be your wife?" she wondered, blunt because that is how it was between them. Honest. How she always wanted it to be. "Would you remarry and try to produce an heir if I agreed to it here and now?"

"Without a second thought, if you said you loved me too."

His swift answer and the tenderness in his eyes made it hard to think.

"Do you love me too, Prudence?" He cupped her cheek as though he thought her precious. "Setting all threat of marriage aside, do you feel how I feel?"

Though tempted to lie in order to keep him at a distance, she would not do that. Never with him.

"I am fairly certain I have loved you from the moment our eyes connected when in my golden gown." Her voice sounded strained to her own ears. "But that changes nothing. Nor will it ever."

"It does not," he agreed, pulling her even closer, his strong arm a possessive cage whether he realized it or not. One that did not make her feel trapped, however. Rather she felt captured in the best way possible.

"If anything, it makes me want to try harder," he went on, his voice gruff as he lowered his lips to hers without kissing her. Barely touching as his voice grew softer. More intense. His words were sensual. Vivid. "If anything, it makes me want to bury myself in you again until you whimper. Lose myself inside you until you have no choice but to be mine."

Her eyes drifted, and her lips tingled at how appealing that sounded. Yet she found her tongue. Said what needed saying. "Even if that takes a lifetime?"

"*Especially* if it takes so long." He brushed his lips across hers. "Over and over and over again."

Before she could respond, he caught her lips with his and kissed her so intensely that her knees weakened, and she melted against him. Desperately wanted him inside her again.

Until another rap came on the door, and Agnus intruded once more. "Dinner is nearly ready, my lady. Your Grace."

"Dinner?" she murmured against his mouth before she put a finger to his lips and mouthed that she would handle this.

She smoothed her hair, made sure her clothing was as it should be, and stepped out of the room, only to find her maid not looking at her sternly but with curiosity. Barely constrained, based on the way Fenwick vanished around the corner as though he had been waiting for news of Prudence and Jacob as well.

"Miss Agnus," she said in greeting.

"My lady." Agnus' hands were clasped in front of her, and her gaze more on the door behind Prudence than on her mistress. "I hope all is going well between you and the duke."

"Very well, thank you." She narrowed her eyes when she swore Fenwick peeked around the corner, then pulled back. "Though I am sorry to say the duke is weary indeed after his travels. If you could see a bath drawn for him and food brought to both of our rooms so we might dine in private, that would be most appreciated. I will also not need assistance undressing and preparing for bed tonight, so you need not attend me."

"Of course, my lady," Agnus said. Fenwick cleared his throat from somewhere unseen, clearly finding the situation more inappropriate than it already was. "I will see to things straight away." She tidied Prudence's dress with a small, unexpected smile, and adjusted a portion which clearly had been pulled down a tad too far. "There are very few of us about this eve with the storm, and all will be below stairs, so if you need assistance, ring your bell. Otherwise, your home is very much your own tonight." She curtsied. "I wish you both a lovely evening and hope the duke catches up on his rest."

When Agnus' eyes rose to her face, she knew her maid was well aware of what had transpired in the study. What would continue to transpire between her and Jacob. More than that, she approved of it. Wanted to see Prudence happy.

"Thank you," she said softly and squeezed her maid's hand because she knew they were beyond employer and employee now. Prudence had a good friend in Agnus. "As always, do not hesitate to enjoy a nice meal yourself." She could not help a small smile. "And do be sure to extend the invitation to those traveling with the duke as well."

"Of course, my lady."

"Oh, and Miss Agnus?"

"Yes, my lady."

"Do see Mr. Fenwick joins everyone else below stairs." She winked. "As I do believe he could use a bit of company and a good night's rest too."

Agnus chuckled and curtsied before she vanished. Just as Prudence did when she showed Jacob to his room.

"Do we have a connecting door then, love?" His amused gaze went from the obvious door between their rooms back to her. "Were you truly *that* bold?"

Rather than respond, she assured him a warm bath would be

brought up soon, and perhaps they could dine together in either of their rooms afterward if he so chose. Before he could reply, she stepped aside as a tub was carried in, then retired to her own room, only to count down the minutes until she saw him again.

Wind howled, and sleet mixed with snow, tapping against the windows, making for a cozy night. Having no interest in the food and drink left for her, she paced in front of the fire before drifting to the door between their rooms. She bit her lower lip. Wrung her hands. It had been long enough to heat water for his bath, so was he undressing at this very moment? If so, what did he look like beneath his clothes? Was his body as strong as it had seemed? His chest as broad? His arousal as sizeable as it had felt?

While curious, she wondered if it were any of her business. She could give him everything but marriage. With that in mind, she could hardly believe he had insinuated he strived for such with her. That he would want her that much. Loved her to that degree.

*Love.*

Did he truly? So fast? As strongly as she felt for him? Because she became more and more sure, that was very much what she felt. This elusive emotion that had plagued her. Teased her. Claimed it existed despite her having no clue what it really meant. What it felt like.

As if he sensed her very thoughts, their adjoining door swung open, and Jacob stood there in all his glory. She barely had a moment to take in a body that was every bit as perfect as she had fantasized before he yanked her into his arms and kissed her soundly.

"How am I ever going to be able to leave you for weeks when minutes felt like hours?" he murmured against her lips. "You have cast a spell on me, lass."

"And you, me," she whispered before their kiss deepened, and she finally touched him as she had long wanted to. He was hard. Hot. So masculine. She groaned in protest when he pulled away, and his gaze roamed her body.

The way he looked at her made her entire body come alive. Made her feel like he saw everything underneath, whether she was clothed or not. Yet she wanted him to see it all, every last bit, so she started undressing, only for him to stop her.

"No, lass." His brogue thickened. Became less aristocratic. "I want to undress you." He came behind her and murmured in her ear. "I want to see you at my leisure. View what I have dreamt about every waking moment since last we met." He nipped her earlobe. "Since I pleasured you hours ago."

She was unsure what made her tremble with awareness more. His erotic words or the excruciatingly slow way he lowered her dress and untied her stays.

"You should enjoy the bath while it is still warm," she managed on a breathy whisper.

"Only if you bathe with me." He swept aside her hair and peppered kisses down the side of her neck. "Will you bathe with me, Prudence?"

Powerless to say no, she murmured *yes* and let her head drop back against his chest as he lowered her dress. She had never felt as adored as she did in his arms. Never so sensual as she did when he tossed aside her stays and lowered her chemise.

"Stunning." He trailed his fingers down her neck and fondled her breasts. The look in his eyes when he returned to her front, lowered her garments entirely, and took her in made her feel incredibly desirable. "If not for your servants' effort to warm the bath water, I would have you in bed already."

She blushed when he fell to a knee, urged her to step out of her dress then started on her shoes and stockings. Never so personal with a man, she tried to remain confident when she felt terribly self-conscious. Randolph had only ever taken her once she was beneath the blankets, so this was most irregular.

Jacob must have sensed her growing unease because his gaze traveled back to her face and lingered. "You truly are beautifully made, my love." He stood and cupped her cheek, making her wholly aware of how aroused he had become. "And I will tell you such until you believe it. Until you no longer feel discomfort in front of me."

Acutely aware of their nude proximity, she swallowed hard. "Was I that obvious?"

He offered no answer other than a soft smile and a gentle kiss.

"Come." Jacob brought her to the tub and stepped in. "Let us bathe so you have time to adjust."

He sat, took her hand, and urged her to sit between his legs. Unbelievably nervous despite what they had shared downstairs, she joined him.

"See, not so bad, aye?" His brogue thickened again as he pulled her back against him, then rested his arms on the sides of the tub. Allowed her to adjust to the position. Which, she could admit, was quite risqué considering his erection rested against her backside.

A sensation she also could admit was not all that terrible.

Nor was the feel of his body when she finally relaxed enough to touch him. Explore him. From the strength of his arms to his muscular thighs. In turn, he did the same to her while chatting. No doubt a means to keep her at ease as he washed first her back, then other parts of her.

"This is supposed to be your bath," she said breathlessly at one point, immersed in how erotic bathing could feel. "Not mine."

"I am seeing to myself well enough." He tilted her head back and poured water over her hair. "And as you say, this is my bath, so I should enjoy it as I see fit, should I not?"

"You should." Pleasurable shivers rippled through her when he kissed the side of her neck again. "As much as possible."

They might have chatted, but she would be unable to say what about. Not when he slid the washcloth slowly over her breasts, then so close to the throbbing juncture between her thighs she squirmed with need. A longing he finally satisfied when his lips found hers again, and he left the cloth behind.

When he stroked her center with his warm fingers.

She moaned against his mouth as he caressed her swollen, sensitive flesh like he had that first night. Painfully slow until he curled two fingers inside her while rubbing her tiny nub. Already so aroused, it took very few strokes before she tumbled over the edge and arched against him.

He grunted with approval and continued kissing her before he started all over again. This time she was able to truly sink into the pleasure. Immerse herself in it as he stroked her breast with his free hand. When he tweaked her nipple while curling his fingers deeper inside her, she clamped down on her lower lip at the exquisite combination of sensations. Ones that became so intense she reached an even higher pinnacle this time and shook with release.

Lost to what spiked through her, she was hardly aware of him lifting her out of the tub. Barely aware of him drying her off. She was, however, fully conscious of him laying her in his bed and coming over her. Very much present when he kissed her deeply, settled between her thighs and thrust deep.

Where downstairs had been an untouchable experience, something about feeling his body against hers when he finally filled her was so much better. So incredible a fresh burst of mini climaxes washed over her.

He made a sound of approval as he continued moving. Slowly at first, staring into her eyes, then faster. Just when she thought he had offered her the ultimate pleasure, she found even more in his arms. This time in a more primal way. One that made her wrap her legs around him and take him even deeper, chasing the sinful feelings he provoked.

Sweat slicked their heated skin as he drove them higher. Love and romance blended with lust and insatiable need. A craving to reach their peak that was so strong it hit them hard when it came. He pressed deep one last time, locked up against her, and groaned into the pillow. She feared she was not so quiet when she shuddered and cried out. It could not be helped, though. Not when unfathomable pleasure speared her, and her surroundings seemed to explode with color.

When his gaze finally found her face again, and he wiped tears from her cheeks, she realized she wept. That he had pulled forth such intense emotions. He said nothing but brushed his lips across hers one more time and tucked her by his side.

They never did eat but dozed off before waking and making love several more times that night. He had a way of stirring her awake with passionate caresses and long deep kisses. Affection that inevitably tangled them up in one another's arms again.

"Do not go, love," he murmured sleepily when she eventually got up to return to her room. "Stay with me."

While her servants undoubtedly knew what was happening up here, she would only push impropriety so far. She cared not what they thought of her actions. Her concern lay more with Jacob. As heartbreaking as the thought, he would have to take a wife someday, and she would not have such precise rumors get back to that woman's ears. Something she made clear when he caught her wrist and pulled her back into his arms.

"You think of someone who will never exist," he said. "Not unless it is you, Prudence." He cupped her cheek and grew most serious. "Say you will marry me, my love, so that you need not run off like this."

He might have alluded to it in the study, but his request was so direct now her heart did a little flip. Yet she forced herself to ignore it. Not just for his sake but for her newly discovered independence.

"I cannot." She unraveled from his embrace lest she risk surrendering to his will. Because he was a force unto himself when he looked at her like that. When he said words she would gladly have said yes to in her youth. "I will see you when you wake, Your Grace."

Before he had a chance to capture her again, she made her way into her room and shut the door. Prayed he did not pursue her. Hoped he understood how much she needed to stay strong now more than ever. Needed to stand her ground so she did not cave into his very convincing words. His equally convincing touch.

Fortunately, he did not follow, and she slid beneath her blankets. As expected, she did not sleep but stared at the door. Waited with nary a breath drawn at points, wondering if he would come through it. If she should want him to.

He never did enter, though, and she eventually got out of bed in the morning and made her way down to breakfast after Agnus helped her dress. Her maid said little, but Prudence could tell by the knowing glances she cast her that she was no fool.

"It seems the duke has decided to stay on for a few days until it is safe enough to travel," Agnus said at one juncture. "In fact, he already awaits you for breakfast."

"Does he, then?" So he was not fleeing? Rushing home now that he had conquered her flesh, then had his marriage proposal denied? Her heart did that strange little somersault it liked to do when it came to him. "Likely sound thinking to stay on until it is safe."

"I agree, my lady." Though faint, she did not miss the amusement in Agnus' voice. "As it were, the short drive to our local inn might prove dangerous indeed."

"Indeed."

She supposed she expected to find him in a mood when she made her way downstairs, yet he seemed in rather pleasant spirits. But then, little did she know he was planning to go to war.

Moreover, that she was his intended prize when he conquered all.

# Chapter Sixteen

J ACOB HAD NOT been fibbing when he made it plain he wanted Prudence as his wife. By his side always. Which meant he intended to win her over at every turn. Make her love him so much she simply could not refuse him in the end.

So he spent the days he could spare away from his estate doing just that. Which simply meant doing what came naturally to them. Talking endlessly. Discussing the history of her estate. Playing cards and other entertaining games.

Making love into the wee hours of each morning.

There was nothing he did not adore about her. From their lively discussions to how she made him laugh to the way she felt in his arms. How he felt in hers. As it happened, she was as curious in bed as she was out of it and wanted to try everything. Feel all the sensations they could pull from one another.

Which in their case seemed endless.

He would have never thought it upon meeting her years ago, but Lady Barrington was creative and adventurous once freed of her sensual inhibitions. Better still, she was as interested in bringing him pleasure as he was her.

"Can you not stay one more day?" Prudence murmured sleepily in the early hours of their last morning together. She dusted talented fingers down his stomach toward an arousal that could not get enough of her. "The roads may be clear, but there still might be a spot of ice or two."

"I would if I could, love." He kissed her temple. "But alas, my kingdom needs its king." He bit back a groan when her hand wandered lower. "As does its queen when she finally gives in and lays her claim."

Prudence said nothing to that, but he knew she would not. She had grown stubbornly committed to the idea there was a mistress better suited to his castle. While it frustrated him, he kept it to himself for no other reason than he would not frighten her off. If that were not trying enough, he also found it impossible to tell her the last secret still lingering between them.

That she had not been the first lass he had helped break free from the trauma of an awful marriage.

He had tried several more times to confess, but again, it never seemed the right moment. Honestly, he wondered how necessary it really was to tell her she wasn't his first. Prudence was doing well. Flourishing, at that. So what did it matter if he had helped other women heal too? She might even find it admirable. Either way, he never did get around to telling her.

Instead, he well and truly lost himself to her.

So when the time came to say goodbye once again, it felt far more difficult than it had at MacLauchlin Castle. Not only because she refused to marry him but because she had come to an unfortunate conclusion.

"I might long to see your estate and gave you my word I would visit, but in light of circumstances, I think it best I stay away, after all," she had said. "While it is one thing to take the chances we did here at my estate, it would be foolhardy to do so at my castle." Her voice had grown softer, as though she loathed saying it but voiced it regardless. "It is far too close to home for you, Jacob. Your future wife does not deserve to begin her reign there, with possible rumors of my previous stay reaching her ears. That said, I feel it best that any future trysts between you and I be here at my manor."

He thought that a terrible idea as it would vastly cut down

how often they saw each other, but she remained stubborn about it. Right to the end as he kissed the back of her hand outside his carriage and longed to pull her into his arms one last time. Hold her until all his duties and obligations faded away and left only her.

"Write me, my love," he murmured in her ear after kissing her cheek. "Write me every day. Twice a day if you can manage."

She blinked back tears and offered a jerky nod. When his carriage finally departed, it was torture. Bittersweet, even though he knew he would be back.

And so their letters began again, starting with the one they had written each other the night before. Only neither possessed the same banter. Instead, there was poignant heartache.

*23 February 1816*

*My Dearest Jacob,*

*This might seem, in its own strange way, more of a goodbye than before, but it is not. Rather, it is a farewell until next we meet. A mere goodbye until you return if you are still in need of female companionship. And always, but always, a welcome haven for a beloved friend.*

*I feel we have found each other in a whole new way. Love each other in a fashion that will sustain no matter its form. So, let our correspondence not be full of heartache but of joy and new beginnings yet again.*

He wondered before he kept reading if those last few smudged words might have been due to a tear.

*Whatever comes of our future going forward, know that I love you. That I will continue sharing my journey in Dalness with you. I will imagine you by my side on grand new adventures and loving and supporting me as you have all along.*

*Until next we meet,*
*Your Loving Prudence*

While he continued writing her daily, he felt many of his letters would make her feel guilty for denying him, so he sent only the ones he deemed appropriate.

*2 March 1816*

*My Dearest Prudence,*

*Apologies that it took so long to write again. As you know from the letter I wrote you our last night together, my love for you is undying and will remain such. Things are busier than ever, but you are never far from my thoughts. You are forever in my heart.*

*I will be embarking on another restoration project soon and long to tell you all about it. I'm eager to hear your thoughts on how I should proceed. In truth, they would be most appreciated as I value your input.*

*Your Loving and Ever Devoted,*
*Jacob*

Interested in her feedback, he attached a form with all the necessary information, including his thoughts.

*21 March 1816*

*My Dearest Jacob,*

*I cannot tell you how much it pleases me that you value my opinion. Upon looking over what you provided, I think you should proceed forward just as planned. You might, however, look into restoring the church, too, as it is the pillar of the community. That said, I could not help but notice the restorations are but a village over from me. Does that mean you will be visiting soon?*

Again the last few words were smudged as though perhaps a tear had fallen.

*In other news, I am pleased to share that my sister, Grace Howard, as well as her husband and wee son, William, recently visited. I believe I mentioned them to you? She is the one Like Maude, she is madly in love with her spouse. Something I could never have imagined before, but thanks to you, I now realize is possible.*

Despite his unending desire to show her such wedded bliss, he kept with the lightheartedness of the letter and smiled at her using the Scottish word *wee*. He imagined that she hesitated before continuing. Saw her trying to figure out just how to word what he had already sensed from her when she spoke of Grace.

> *It was poor of me not to visit with her and her family all these years. Especially my beautiful nephew. He is no longer the baby I once knew but a lovely, well-mannered eight-year-old boy. I suspect, however, he has a free spirit much like my sister, his aunt Abby, or Lady Abigail, if you will. Might it never be suppressed as I know hers has been by a husband three times her age.*
> *Please do write me back soon of your restoration plans and where they might lead you. I eagerly await word.*
> *Your Loving Prudence*

Despite the words, why did her closure somehow seem less loving? Had someone else caught her eye? As he originally set out to do, had Jacob merely been the healing balm between her late husband and a true and lasting love to come? A man who would not crave to make her his permanently but be content to love her from afar?

*27 March 1816*

*My Dearest Prudence,*

*I have taken your advice and decided not only to see to the restorations in the village near you but intend to restore the church as well.*

And because he hated to assume when she could very well

have taken another lover.

*I might be there several weeks, so I intend to get a room at the nearby inn. It is my fondest hope that I will see you. That perhaps you might even join me when visiting the village as the work begins? For where would I be without my dearest friend and all her savvy advice? Until next we meet, my fair commander.*

*Your Beloved Jacob*

*8 April 1816*

*My Dearest Second-in-Command,*

*Nonsense! You will not stay at an inn! I demand you return to your liege and rest comfortably in her castle. I will not take no for an answer. As to helping you oversee restorations, nothing would make me happier. I eagerly await news of your arrival.*

*Your Ever Faithful and Loving, Prudence*

His gaze lingered on those last words. How she always seemed to sense his thoughts and even insecurities despite the distance. But then he supposed he did the same with her. Had done since the very beginning.

While they continued corresponding, between running his estate and putting together such a venture, he was not en route to Dalness until mid-May. It had been more than three long months since they last saw each other, and he was beyond desperate to hold her again. Feel her warmth. Love her as only he could.

As it had been the first time he had arrived at her manor, she greeted him at his coach. Only this go around, she was alone and did not wait for him to step out. Rather she asked Donal to give them a moment alone, then crawled into the carriage and sat next to Jacob with a wide smile.

"Foolish woman." He pulled her onto his lap. "You know better than to sit there when you should be sitting here."

Wise enough to understand they needed a moment alone, his

footman closed the door before Jacob closed his mouth over hers. Kissing her again felt like coming home. Exactly where he was always meant to be.

"My lady," he eventually murmured against her lips before he lost control and took her here and now. "You have become quite forward of late."

"I have, Your Grace." She wore a soft smile when she looked at him. "Does that bother you?"

He was tempted to comment that perhaps yes, if she had met another and was equally forthright with the sod but dispelled the notion when she continued.

"Does it bother you when I am all yours until you find the future Duchess of Argyll?" she murmured before kissing him again.

Before making it clear he need never fear her giving herself to another.

"When are you going to understand *you* are the future Duchess of Argyll?" he said.

Naturally, she made no comment but continued kissing him until they finally found their way out of the carriage.

"I thought you were rather fond of the room you stayed in before." She offered him a small, knowing smile. "So I had it prepared for you again."

"Thank you, my lady." Desperate for every night they would spend together over the next few weeks, he met her smile. "I seem to remember that room had an especially pleasing view."

He enjoyed the way her cheeks pinkened at the implication.

"You must have left at quite the hour to get here so early," she said. "It is a lovely day. Might we enjoy a picnic, or would you prefer to rest?"

He suspected, by the wicked twinkle in her eyes, she had more in mind than a picnic. "A picnic would be lovely."

Her butler opened the door and bowed. "Your Grace."

"Mr. Fenwick." He nodded hello to Agnus when she curtsied. "Miss Agnus."

Where he thought they might take a few moments alone in the study, instead, Prudence urged him to get settled in while Agnus saw to a basket. "I will await you in the gardens, Your Grace, then we will go from there."

He found it not just refreshing but nostalgic to be back in her manor. Surrounded by her sweet scent. Every room he passed brought back warm memories of time spent with her.

Especially his room.

His gaze lingered on the bed. He still saw her sprawled out on it. Remembered how she had taken him between her thighs. Into her body. Thoughts he tried his hardest to push aside lest a stubborn arousal keep her waiting.

As promised, he found her in the gardens. And, as always, the sight of her took his breath away. She might have been beautiful when he met her, but now she was truly stunning. Beyond radiant in her happiness. Impossible to look away from as yellow and purple crocus and pink cherry blossoms bloomed on either side of her.

"My love," he said softly when he joined her. He clenched his fist lest he cup her soft cheek where others could see. Rather, he took the basket from her to occupy himself. "I cannot tell you how difficult it is not to pull you back into my arms at this very moment. How frustrating that I cannot kiss you at will."

"Then let us walk until you can." She linked arms with him. "There is a lovely spot I have wanted to take you to since I found it."

They were about to continue on when Donal caught up with them.

"My lady." His valet bowed from the waist and handed her a folded blanket for them to sit on while eating. "Miss Agnus wanted me to give you this."

"Thank you, Mr. Donal." A warm smile curled her mouth. "We will be gone for several hours. I encourage you to enjoy the beautiful day. Perhaps join Miss Agnus on a stroll?"

Jacob bit back amusement when Donal's eyebrows swept up.

He seemed unsure how to respond. Had that been a suggestion or a request? Having clearly decided it best to go with the latter, his valet finally found his tongue.

"Yes, my lady." He offered another quick bow. "Straight away."

While Jacob had been unable to get much out of Donal about his interactions with Prudence's maid during their last visit here, it seemed Agnus implied there might have been a truce. It was hard to tell with those two, and he said as much when he and Prudence set out.

"Actually, I have news on that front since last we wrote." She gave him a co-conspirator look. The corner of her mouth notched. "I heard from a chambermaid who heard from a footman that when your letters arrived, there was also one for Miss Agnus."

"Indeed?" Donal, that old bugger. "From my valet, then?"

"She could not say only that Miss Agnus seemed quite eager to receive it."

"Well, that is certainly telling." Reflecting on how changed Prudence was from the haughty lass who would not even acknowledge a servant, much less gossip with them, he grinned. "Might I ask how you heard such from a chambermaid?"

"I have my ways." Her eyes sparkled. "Besides, it is not all that hard to discover secrets around here. It seems much like high society, simple Scottish folk know much about everything. Not to say they are simple because they are anything but. Rather, I have come to enjoy the friends I have made in these parts."

"So you said in your letters." They started down a sun-dappled path. "And I cannot tell you how happy that makes me. How happy I am you have found such a good life here." He had said it before but wanted to make things clear one more time. "As you know, your estate would always be here if we married. A retreat that you could visit often and at will."

"Yet not live at," she reminded softly. "For a duchess must be there for her people every bit as much as their duke."

She was right. Her presence would be required but not as frequently as she seemed to think, and he had said that before too. While tempted to keep at the matter, he would not mar the perfect afternoon nor their first moments together after so much time apart.

So he steered them back to a lighter conversation and simply enjoyed her company. Lingered on her every word. Adored the sound of her laughter. Basked in the feel of having her so close again. Soon enough, the same wicked twinkle that had been in her eyes when she initially suggested this stroll reappeared, and he asked her about it.

"I could not help but reflect on a fantasy I once had," she confessed readily enough. "One I had before coming upon you and Emma strolling in the hedge gardens at MacLauchlin Castle."

"I dare say." He stopped her. "You fantasized about me so soon?"

Her gaze grew almost sultry. "I did." She perked a brow. "Would you like to hear about it?"

More than words could express. "Very much so."

"Well," she gestured at a small grassy, sunlit clearing cushioned between trees, "I imagined we might come upon a spot much like that one. When we did, you might pull me against you, cup my cheek and kiss me. Then, once our passion became too much, you might sweep me off my feet and lay me down in that bit of grass. I think you can probably imagine the rest from there."

"I very much can." Never so eager, he set down the basket and blanket and reeled her against him. "More than that, I intend to see it through."

# Chapter Seventeen

PRUDENCE HAD LONGED for this moment since she discovered the sunlit woodland oasis so similar to what she fantasized about. Longed for when Jacob pulled her into his arms and kissed her as hungrily as she had envisioned. Kissed her with so much passion it put her imagination to shame.

As did the feeling of being swept up in his arms and laid in the warm grass. Where things had gone slower in her fantasy, reality proved more frenzied. Her fanciful imagination could never have foreseen how much she would need him inside her again. The near-crazed desperation they would feel when his lips found hers again and removing clothing became the last thing on their minds.

Instead, upon her insistence that she could not wait a moment longer, Jacob hiked up her skirts, freed himself, and entered her. They both groaned at the feel of it. The incredible sensation of coming back together this way after so long.

"Bloody hell, lass," he breathed, cupping her cheek again. His lustful gaze roamed her face. Lingered on her eyes. "How is it you feel better and better every time? Better when you felt so verra incredible our first time?"

She tried to respond, but the words died on her lips when he thrust again. When she gave herself over to how he made her feel. He had a way of moving against her that elicited intense pleasure. First between her thighs until it expanded into her womb, then fanned out to her outermost extremities.

"Jacob," she moaned, arching into the feeling. "My love."

He seemed to like that endearment because he moved harder. Faster. Deeper if possible until he pressed so deeply neither could hold back any longer, and they found release at the same time. Found such intense gratification, they trembled against each other and struggled to catch their breath.

Eventually, he adjusted their clothing, lay back in the grass, and wrapped his arm around her when she rested her cheek on his chest. Cherished the beat of his heart. She had thought herself quite the modern woman and free thinker refusing his marriage proposal and having such a scandalous affair, but truth be told, their time apart had become incredibly difficult. She loved all she had found here in Dalness, but there was a hole in her heart when he was not here. A void no amount of freedom and happiness could fill.

How could it when he was her greatest love and dearest friend?

They lay there for a while, simply holding each other before he spread out the blanket and took her much more languidly. Removed her clothing like unwrapping a precious gift. Kissed her from head to toe before flipping her onto her stomach and starting all over again.

Ready for him, so eager it hurt, she propped her backside up enough that he could slide into her all over again. Make her groan as he braced himself up with one arm, gripped her hip with his free hand, and thrust in such a way he hit particularly sensitive areas. Ones that had her sobbing from the sheer ecstasy of it.

Pleasure so intense it almost felt painful.

Right there with her, feeling the same building euphoria, he lowered even more, his front flush with her back, and moved slower. Deeper. With long, intense strokes that made her seize up and let go seconds later. In turn, he trembled, groaned, and released as well, pulsing inside her in a way she could never get enough of.

They stayed that way for a time, lost in how they made one another feel before they dressed and enjoyed a light lunch along with a bottle of claret. Soon enough, they were laughing and chatting as they always did. And such did not stop over the duration of his stay. More than that, as expected, the gap in her life fell away, and everything was absolutely perfect.

In fact, they were the best two weeks of her life.

They spent their evenings enjoying each other's company and making love. Their days overseeing restorations in the nearby village. As promised, he involved her in everything, and she adored every minute. He also taught her to fish in their spare time. A wonderful pastime she enjoyed more than expected.

"I cannot tell you how much I have cherished this time," she said as they left the village on the last day. "I shall think of all we accomplished here whenever I visit." Rather than have him see how sad she had become, she looked out his carriage window and blinked back tears. "It has been a most delightful and worthwhile project."

"It has." Clearly aware of her distress, Jacob pulled her onto his lap and cupped the side of her neck, so she had no choice but to look at him. "What is it, my love?"

"You know full well what it is." She pressed her lips together when they wobbled and tried to gather herself. "I have had such a lovely time and loathe to see it come to an end."

"Then we should do this again," he said softly, wiping away an escaped tear. "We shall restore the whole of Scotland together if that is your wish."

"I would like that." A lump formed in her throat. "But these things tend to take time to put together. Time to..."

Jacob seemed to understand what she was really trying to say because he rested her cheek against his chest, stroked her hair, and let her weep. She knew she was the only one standing in the way of being with him always. Of feeling this immense happiness all the time.

The months between seeing him had become more than torturous. She suffered such melancholy after he left in February and suspected it would be worse this time. That she might never recover. And that undoubtedly translated later that night when they made love. In the heartfelt passion between them as they came together time and time again.

"We cannot keep on like this." He rubbed her back to soothe her when she found herself adrift in melancholy once more. Spent from lovemaking, she remained partially draped over him. "I cannot bear it any more than you. To that end, you must stop second-guessing this."

Her heart seemed to stop in her chest. Was he ending things? Could she blame him if he did?

"I understand," she whispered, her voice useless. Fear and sadness washed over her.

"I do not think you do." He adjusted their position until he could see her face. "You are not supposed to feel this anguish any more than I, Prudence. It implies we are meant to be together always. So I beg you to think long and hard about my proposal. More so than I suspect you already have." He traced her eyebrow and trailed his finger along her jawline. The pain in his eyes reflected what he felt. "I am so incredibly in love with you, lass, and that will never change." He hesitated a moment. "But I fear you are caging yourself in yet again by not doing what you truly want."

Before she could counter him, he went on. Repeated what he had already made clear. "We both know marriage to me would not be the rhetorical cage you suffered with your late husband. What is happening to you now, however, to *us*, the moment we separate, feels like the worst kind of prison, does it not?" He shook his head. "Surely, you feel it too. The way everything grows duller when we are not together. The sense of loss when we reach out for each other at night only to find our arms empty? The ache of not being able to hold one another when we want to?"

She felt all those things and more. And they did, in some strange way, feel much like the place she had been in with Randolph. A cage of sorts only this time, as he said, of her own making.

"As you know, the MacLauchlins have invited us to their Midsummer Day ball next month," he went on. "Might you take the time in between to give us a great deal of thought, my love? Consider finally accepting my proposal? I will not take another and continue as we are as long as you will have me, but it grows more and more difficult. Is this the newly minted cage you want to live out your days in? *Our* days?"

She tried to answer but could not because the same old fear got in the way.

"Take this month." He brushed his lips across hers. "And think. *Truly* think."

"I will," she said before she could stop herself. But she meant it. She would. Had to. Because she could only imagine how difficult things would become if they continued doing this over the years. If her heart hurt this badly now, how would it feel a year from now? Five years? Longer?

As anticipated, his departure the next morning was unspeakably difficult. Thankfully, Agnus and Fenwick, who had become great companions in their own way, were right there with her. Agnus kept her elbow locked with Prudence's as Fenwick opened all the doors and made sure Agnus got her tucked into bed after Jacob left.

"You cannot keep doing this to yourself, my lady." Agnus sat by her side. "It is clear how much you love your duke. How much he loves you."

"I thought I was so strong," she whispered. "But I have never felt so weak."

"Then perhaps it is time to focus on what will make you strong again, my lady." Agnus squeezed her hand. "Because you do truly excel at such."

She appreciated the support and said as much before she

closed her eyes and tried to push past the heartache. Something that took time. Even so, she overcame her melancholy the best she could and continued writing Jacob. Kept cherishing his return letters. Found her way back to better and better spirits. But then, a growing sense of certainty had started to take root. Jacob was right. She had put herself in another cage. One lined with fears born of her late husband.

One that could not see freedom and marriage go hand and hand.

What Jacob offered her was something entirely different, though. A bigger freedom. A fresh start. Not trapped in a loveless, cruel marriage but something far different. There would be obligations inherent to taking on the role of a duchess, but she would not be trapped under his ever-watchful eye. Never shunned if she failed. Never left to wonder who he was off bedding.

Jacob was much different than Randolph. Ten times the man. A hundred times. What a true husband should be. She cared naught for his title but everything for him. So what held her back?

Nothing but her, and she had grown quite tired of it.

"I have given it much thought, and I do believe I shall accept a certain proposal at the MacLauchlin's ball, Miss Agnus," she said as her maid prepared her for bed nearly a month later. "I think it is long past the time I realize all the facets of my strength. That said, I can be just as strong with love by my side as I can with it hours away."

Agnus nodded with approval and smiled. "I am truly glad to hear that, my lady."

She met her maid's smile and considered how she might dress for the ball but did not have to think long. "I would like to have the golden gown Lady MacLauchlin gave me prepared as soon as possible." She wrung her hands and frowned at Agnus. "Do you think there will be enough time, as I have rather pushed it to the last minute?"

"I suspect there will be, my lady." Agnus opened the armoire and presented her dress. "As I saw it properly prepared weeks ago."

"Oh, you delightful woman." She fingered the delicate material and bit back tears when she remembered the way Jacob had looked at her in this. How he had pulled her into his arms on the dance floor. She embraced Agnus before her maid knew what was coming. "Thank you, my friend. Thank you more than you know."

"Of course, my lady." Agnus tentatively embraced her back. "May you find all the happiness you deserve."

She very much imagined she would and could not wait to give Jacob her answer. As it turned out, she received a letter from him just before she departed, so she read it in the carriage as they traveled.

*23 June 1816*

*My Dearest Love and Fair Commander,*

*I count down the days until I see you again at MacLauchlin Castle, where it all truly began for us. I long to hear what you have decided. Pray you will finally say yes, so we need not suffer this terrible heartache anymore.*

*Therefore, I propose we go about things in a certain way. We shall come together at the ball like we did the first time. Dance, eat, and enjoy one another's company. I believe it was the eleventh hour when we met atop our battlement, so let that be our place again, but only if you are there to tell me you will become my wife. My duchess. My dearest friend who will always stand by my side. Who might never second guess her lord when he only wants the very best for her.*

*Your beloved Second-in-Command and Lasting Love,*
*Jacob*

Wishing her carriage could cross Scotland in the blink of an eye, she wiped away a tear and gazed out the window. Longed for the moment Jacob saw her in her golden gown again. Craved the second she met him on the battlements and told him she would become his wife.

"Dear sister, welcome back," Maude gushed the moment she arrived and stepped out of her carriage. She threw her arms around Prudence and held on tight. "I am so glad you came. How I have missed you."

"And I, you." She smiled at Maude. "Has our dear sister, Grace, arrived yet? I received a letter that she would be joining us."

"I am afraid not." Worry knit Maude's brow. "It seems her husband, Lord Howard, has fallen ill. To be expected, she wishes to remain by his side until he recovers, which her doctor has assured her will be the case."

"Dear, me, of course." Hopefully, his doctor was right. She could not imagine anything happening to her brother-in-law. Grace would be devastated. Inconsolable.

"So good to see you again, dear friend," Emma said, joining them. She embraced Prudence as well, then pulled back and held her at arm's length. Gazed at her with approval. "I thought you much changed when last we visited, but I see you have changed even more." She issued a smile, her innuendo about Jacob obvious. "Scotland and all its wonders truly do agree with you."

"They very much do." She met her friend's smile. "It has been such an incredible year, thanks to you, Lady Campbell."

"Oh, I imagine I had little to do with it." Emma's smile turned knowing. "But very much you finding the independence you so richly deserve." She squeezed Prudence's hand. "And I cannot tell you how happy I am at how everything has progressed in your life. Hope that you continue finding happiness in all things."

"I very much intend to." She wished she could scream out loud how she felt. What she was about to do. Instead, as more and more people arrived, she could only hope Emma saw her happiness and understood her returned innuendo. "This very night..." she let her words linger a moment, "when I enjoy the ball, of course."

Emma's eyes sparkled with pleasure. She nodded to let Prudence know she understood. "I could not be more pleased to hear that, Lady Barrington."

They had little time to talk after that as things grew too busy. Not before Emma had a chance to send Prudence in the right direction, though. "I know you have had little time to hear the news, but I am so pleased to share that the Duke of Argyll has joined us for the celebrations. Do be sure to say hello to him in the drawing room."

Just like every time she knew he was close, her heart leapt, and she wanted to race into his waiting arms. Because she suspected they would be open, be damned decorum. Yet as Mr. Fenwick would primly say, and he was right, there was such a thing as proper manners, and she must abide by them. Now more than ever, if she were to become a duchess.

So she allowed the butler, dear Finley, to take her coat and made her way toward the drawing room. As always, when she knew he was close, it felt like she walked on air. Floated. Especially when she arrived at the door and spied him standing in front of the fire, chatting with several gentlemen. Better still, finally saw him as he was meant to be.

# Chapter Eighteen

JACOB SWORE HE felt Prudence before he saw her appear at the door of the drawing room. When their gazes caught, everything faded away, and he could only see her. Only ever her.

She had come.

She was here.

In truth, he had been worried she might not, considering he had given her an ultimatum of sorts. How could he not when the way things were now had become so hard? Torture for them both. Dressed smartly in a lovely blue dress suited to traveling, Prudence seemed frozen in place until Maude and Blake nudged her along.

"Oh, how wonderful that we are all together again." Maude grinned back and forth between Jacob and Prudence when the three of them joined him. "A bit of a full circle, is it not?"

"It is," Jacob said once he found his voice. What was it about Prudence that made every time feel like the first? He let his lips linger on the back of her hand when he kissed it. Remembered kissing other parts of her. Tasting her in the throes of passion. "So good to see you again, Lady Barrington."

"You as well, Your Grace." Prudence curtsied, and her cheeks turned rosy. Almost as if she reflected on their lovemaking every bit as much. "Such a pleasure."

Silence stretched as he kept her hand and their gazes held.

What he would not do to be alone with her right now. To pull her into his arms and kiss her senseless. Kiss her until she told him what he longed to hear.

*"Of course, I will marry you, my dearest Jacob,"* she would murmur *softly in a way that told him she wanted him between her thighs soon. "How foolish of me to have put you off for so long."*

"Your Grace?" Blake asked, tearing him from his reverie.

"Aye?" he asked, startled.

"Might we sit and enjoy refreshments before you return to business?"

He glanced around only to recall they were not alone, and thoughts of Prudence moaning as he took her were highly inappropriate. So he joined her on the sofa where they had sat the first day. Chatted as if everything that happened between then and now never transpired.

Only it had, and he felt it every time Prudence glanced his way.

"I must say, I quite like seeing you in your plaid, Your Grace," she said softly when Maude and Blake were distracted. "It suits you so very well."

"Thank you, my lady." Caught in the sheer impact of seeing her again, he had forgotten this would be the first time she saw him in full Highland regalia outside of a portrait. The holiday called for it, so he had dressed appropriately.

If they had been alone, he would have answered in any number of ways. How pleased he was that she liked it. That he would live in his tartan if she wished it. Die in it if she asked him to as long as she were by his side wearing his clan's colors as well.

"How were your travels here, my lady?" he asked at one point during their very proper conversation. Ever-so-discreetly, he rested his thigh against hers. "Comfortable, I trust?" He longed to know if she were here for all the right reasons. "That you enjoyed the journey and had time to contemplate all the wonders of our beloved county?"

"I most certainly did, Your Grace." Her lovely gaze never left his face as she sipped her tea. "Fortunately, there was no need to contemplate as I am well aware how wondrous Scotland and her people are."

Did that mean she would be saying yes? He could only pray.

They kept on with double innuendoes and wordplay for some time before they inevitably eased into their usual way when together. Comfortable and chatty. While he wanted to steal her away up to the battlements, they had made a deal. The eleventh hour this eve, and she would give him her answer. Although equally tempted to pull her off into the nearest hideaway and at least kiss her hello, the hour was wearing on. He still had business to attend to, and she needed to prepare for the ball.

So he bid her farewell, his thoughts forever with her as he used Blake's study and saw to things. He focused enough to accomplish his tasks, but it was bloody difficult. Should he find a way up to her? Sneak into her room and make love to her before the busy hours ahead?

Jacob was hardly aware of Blake entering once he concluded his business. Rather, he had rested his head back against his chair, closed his eyes, and tried to remain calm. Level minded when he felt anything but.

"It looks like you could use a drink, old chap."

He opened his eyes, grateful when Blake poured him a whisky and sat across from him. Well aware of how far Jacob and Prudence had come and what this night meant, his friend held up his glass. "Here is to receiving the answer you long for this eve, my friend."

"God willing." Jacob toasted him back. "Because I dread what might become of things if I do not."

His time apart from Prudence had become unbearable, so he had no choice but to push her to the edge. Make her see that their pain would only grow worse. The weeks they spent apart last month made that clear. They simply could not bear to be separated. Letters were not nearly enough anymore.

"I cannot think Lady Barrington would say anything but yes,"

Blake said, drawing him back to the present. "Maude is convinced of it. She is already whispering of her plans for your wedding." He winked. "You might have your own plans but know my Maude is bound to offer all sorts of advice."

Jacob forced himself to smile because Maude deserved nothing less. "And she would be welcome to help her sister in every way possible."

"Here, here." Blake's toast was more reserved this time as he considered Jacob. "You have found true love again, friend. Trust that. Know she will say yes because it is clear she loves you just as deeply."

While appreciative of Blake's reassurance, it did not ease his discomfort. Rather, he continued to feel on edge. Desperate in a way he had not quite felt up until this point. What if she said no? If they spent the rest of their lives seeing each other when he could get away? Forever hiding their love?

An emotion only punctuated when she drifted down the stairs hours later wearing the same golden dress she had worn the night they fell in love. While she was every bit as beautiful, she once again had a new radiance about her. One that made all heads turn her way. How could they not when she seemed aglow?

Any thought of being discreet vanished when he met her at the bottom of the stairs. Their gazes connected just as they had before, only this time with certain, undeniable love between them. He offered his arm. "Lady Barrington?"

"Your Grace."

Prudence's gaze never left his face as she curtsied and accepted his arm. Neither said a word as he led her through the crowd and entered the ballroom. Just like before, he swirled her onto the dance floor into a waltz. When he pulled her into his arms, it yet again felt like they had been dancing together their whole lives. As lost on the dance floor as they were when they made love, they swirled round and round without taking their eyes off of each other.

When the music eventually switched to a more lively country dance, they retired to enjoy the festivities. As this was primarily a fire festival, a great deal of the celebrations were out back, where a sizeable bonfire burned, so they headed that way.

"Do tell, what are they doing?" She took in those walking animals around the flames once they arrived outside. "I am unfamiliar with this tradition."

"They are blessing both the beasts and crops," he said. "Further into the highlands, you might come upon people jumping over the fire. Folklore suggests the height reached by the most athletic jumper will be the height of that year's harvest."

"That sounds rather dangerous." She considered the flames and winced. "I do hope the fires they jump are smaller."

"They are." He chuckled. "As most wait until the flames die down before jumping, then head home at sunrise."

"Ah, much safer."

He tried to steer clear of the topic but could not seem to help himself. "Did you know June is the most popular time for weddings here in Scotland?"

"I did not." A promising twinkle lit her eyes. "Do tell."

"Well, this time of year falls between the planting and harvesting of crops, leaving those who work the land time to relax, therefore time for a wedding."

"That makes sense." Naturally, she had her own tidbit of knowledge. "I do know that the first moon of June is called the 'honey moon' because many believed it was the best time to take honey from beehives."

"It is." He bit back a smile. Had that been her way of hinting they would soon be enjoying a honeymoon? She did have a clever way with words, after all.

"Did you know that lasses traditionally gather herbs and flowers on summer solstice day and place them under a pillow in the hopes of important dreams?" He looked at her in a way she could not mistake. "Especially dreams about future lovers."

"Do they?" she said softly. Her gaze lingered on his face. "I suppose that is one tradition I must pass on then, for I suspect flowers have been under my pillow since last November."

"I can only hope." He longed to pull her into his arms so the world might know she was his. "Suffice it to say, love is a common theme at gatherings such as this. Paired sweethearts leap over fires hand in hand or throw flowers across the flames to each other."

"Dear me." Her eyes rounded. "You Scots do like your fire jumping."

"So it seems." He chuckled again. "Rest assured, that is one tradition I will not ask of you."

"Most kind of you, Your Grace." She smiled warmly as they strolled arm in arm past merry goers. "Tell me more of this eve. What I might expect."

He would much prefer to know what he could expect.

"Let me see." He thought about it. "Perhaps something more fantastical in nature?"

"Why not?"

"Well, some say on Midsummer Eve, the veil between this world and the next is especially thin, and powerful forces are abound," he said. "Hundreds of years ago, vigils were held on this night. Rituals at sacred sites, so one might gain the powers of a bard." He flinched. "On the downside, you could also end up utterly mad, dead, or spirited away by fairies."

"Oh, my." Her eyes rounded again. A smile hovered on her mouth. "I suppose we must steer clear of rituals this evening, then."

"Agreed." Unless she considered accepting a marriage proposal ritualistic. "Let us get some food and drink."

MacLauchlin Castle put on a grand affair at this time of year, so there were vendors selling Pontefract cakes and nut-shaped marzipan, as well as a variety of beverages. He grinned when she opted to try ale again.

"Are you starting a tradition with me, my lady?" he teased. "That we might enjoy a token ale at Scottish festivals."

"Would that be so terrible?"

"If anything, it would be preferable," he said. "As Scottish festivals are more frequent than you might think."

"So I have heard."

Which would mean they would need to be around each other more often. Preferably residing under the same roof. Something he suspected she understood as their gazes lingered on one another. Surely, she was going to say yes. She had seemed to hint at it several times.

While he very much enjoyed her company, the eleventh hour could not come soon enough. With the understanding she was to meet him on the battlements rather than walk up with him, the time finally came for them to part ways.

"Might I see you again soon enough, my love," he murmured in her ear. "And may it be with the answer I long for."

"We shall see, Your Grace." Yet the lingering look she gave him was more than promising. The light in her eyes telling.

So he went his own way for the remaining half hour, then headed up to the battlements. It was the first time he had been there since the night they first kissed. How far they had come since then. How much love they had found.

The moment she said yes because he was certain she would, he would scoop her up and take her somewhere private to make love. To finally come together, knowing they could be together that way every night soon after.

In fact, he hoped she would return to his castle with him after the celebrations wrapped up here. They would post banns right away, then marry as soon as possible. She would make a stunning bride. He could already see her shining with the same happiness and love he felt.

She had not arrived on the battlements yet, so he stood where they had that first night looking down on the drawbridge. Remembered how wondrous she had seemed about everything. How she had felt in his arms when he came behind her and pointed down at the darkened forest beyond the torchlight.

It took him a moment to realize there was movement down there. Not at the forest's edge but on the drawbridge. He blinked, hardly believing his eyes. It could not be. Surely he was not seeing straight. Yet he was, and his heart sank. How else could it be when Prudence's carriage had just traveled beneath the portcullis and vanished into the night?

Not only did it seem she would not be accepting his marriage proposal, but worse yet, she was ending their liaison.

# Chapter Nineteen

Just when Prudence thought she could not be happier with Jacob, he proved her wrong. Every moment with him was a delight. Even so, she had been counting down the minutes until they went their separate ways by the bonfire. While a lovely evening, she was eager to reunite with him on the battlements. To finally say yes, she would become his wife. As soon as humanly possible.

Preferring to be alone, she found her way back to the room they had been whisked into the night Elizabeth's piano had been carried down the hallway. She was pleased to find it empty so she might reminisce in peace. How far they had come since then. From disliking one another to finding such incredible love.

She was about to sit in front of the fire but hesitated when she heard someone say her name in conversation. By the sounds of it, two women walked down the hallway, talking about her and Jacob.

"I must say, our handsome duke has done it again," one said. "Did you see how radiant Lady Barrington looked on his arm? Of all people!"

"I did," the other replied. "And I quite admire him for pushing past her horrible name-calling years ago and helping such a prudish woman become what she is now. But then our hero does have a way about him."

"Indeed he does." The first voice dropped an octave, but Prudence still heard her. "How many is this now?"

"How many lovers has he taken since his beloved wife passed?" Based on her hesitation, the second woman seemed to give it some thought. "Quite a few, I would say. And what lucky women they were."

Prudence put a hand to her stomach when nausea welled. She could not be hearing correctly.

"Are they so lucky, though?" the first wondered. "I am told several fell in love with him after he cured them of whatever ill-treatment they had suffered at their late husband's hands. They went their own way afterward, but at what cost? Were they truly cured of their melancholy after such a man, never mind a duke, bedded then left them?"

Prudence struggled to keep listening, but they drifted out of earshot.

"Good lord, no." Struggling to see through tears, she sank down against the wall and tried to make sense of what she had just overheard.

What had Jacob done?

How *could* he?

She was not sure what broke her heart more. That he would do such to another woman or that he had very clearly done the same to her. Now she knew chances were slim that he was actually on their battlement. And if he were, how could she ever go to him now? His behavior sickened her. The idea that he had bedded so many, and likely claimed he loved them just as much as her.

"*Blast* you." It felt like the world crashed down around her. Although inclined to give in to more tears, she needed to temper her emotions until she was out of there. Could she, though? Was such possible when everything around her seemed to have lost its vibrancy? When she felt so utterly heartbroken?

Fortunately, an old, all-too-familiar feeling crept into her veins—iciness she never thought she would feel again. The sort that had sustained her for years when coping with Randolph's infidelity. Detachment, she forced herself to embrace so she could get out of the castle and on her way back home.

To that end, she gathered herself and glared at the chair Jacob had sat in the evening he'd first begun to swindle her. She had been right all along when calling him Rothesay the Scoundrel. He might not have been when Elizabeth still lived but certainly was after she'd passed.

Prudence was not so foolish to think he had not truly loved his late wife but found his behavior afterward detestable. What game had he been playing? Still played? While part of her wanted to confront him, a larger part refused to lay eyes on him again and refused to try navigating more lies, as she suspected he was quite adept at them.

Knew firsthand he was.

No, her days of dealing with lying men were over. She was not that woman anymore. She had found her footing and could not be bothered. Men who behaved like Jacob were beneath her despite how much she loved him.

So, rhetorical armor at the ready, she squared her shoulders and made her way to Finley, grateful when she did not cross paths with anyone she knew.

"I am not feeling well, so I would have you do me a favor, Finley," she said. "I do not want the MacLauchlins or Campbells bothered with my departure. Rather, if you would have Mrs. Agnus see to my belongings and have my carriage brought around while I wait, that would be best."

Clearly concerned, he nodded that he would see to her wishes, hoped she felt better and opened the door for her. She was never so grateful that things were seen to swiftly, and her carriage set out soon after.

"What is it, my lady?" Agnus said gently once they left the castle behind. "Why are we really leaving so quickly?"

"It does not matter." Now there was no risk of encountering anyone, the walls she had so quickly resurrected crumbled once more as she stared out the window and blinked back tears.

"Oh, dear me." Agnus moved until she sat beside Prudence rather than across from her and took her hand. "What happened, my lady?"

Where she would have stiffened away from Agnus' touch a year ago, she was not that woman anymore. So she rested her head on her friend's shoulder and wept until she was finally able to share everything she had overheard.

"I have no words." Agnus' heart was in her eyes. "Other than it does not seem possible of the duke. He seemed too kind a man. Too much in love with you to ever treat you like that. Too decent a person to have ever done such to women before you."

"Yet he did," she whispered and closed her eyes. "I wish to sleep now, Agnus. Sleep until I am able to make my way free of all this."

"I understand but feel I should tell you something first." Agnus sounded tentative. "Perhaps, in some way, it might help."

"And what is that?"

"I have more letters from the duke," Agnus said. "A whole box of them. Ones he never sent, but we felt you should have so you understood just how much he adores you."

"We?" She opened her eyes and frowned. "Whatever do you mean by that?"

Agnus hesitated a moment before she cleared her throat and finally confessed to what Prudence and Jacob had suspected.

"Where I found Mr. Donal quite displeasing upon our first encounters—" she actually blushed—"we have since grown quite fond of one another, my lady."

"Have you?" Despite her grief, she could not help but be happy for her maid. "I am so glad to hear that. He is a fine fellow, my friend." She realized how difficult what had happened might make things going forward, so said what needed saying. "I beg of you, do not let what transpired between the duke and me stand between you two. You should be with Mr. Donal if you have found love. I will dismiss you as soon as we get home with a glowing recommendation and see a carriage bring you to the duke's castle straight away."

"You will do no such thing." Agnus seemed taken aback. "I am your lady's maid and housekeeper. I will not abandon you. Moreover, I am your friend, am I not?"

"You are."

"Then that is that." Agnus shook her head once. "I will stay and hear no more about it." She paused a moment. "Though I dare say it would do my heart good if you would at least read the duke's letters. For me, if no one else."

She narrowed her eyes. "That sounds suspiciously like a thinly veiled condition."

"I would never," Agnus admonished, yet a little gleam lit her eyes. "I just think perhaps it would be good to hear what he had to say. For it was clearly things some part of him wanted you to know."

The idea of reading another one of his letters was heartbreaking, and she said so. Yet the look in Agnus' eyes touched her. As did her willingness to stay on a while as it would not be indefinite. Prudence would convince her to go to Donal. She would make a point of it.

"If you give me some time first," she finally said, biting back more tears. "I will. But make no mistake, it will be for you, and you alone." Eyes narrowed, she considered her maid. "Might I ask why Mr. Donal was traveling with a box of unread letters from the duke?"

"I do not know, my lady," Agnus said. "Other than I suspect he wanted you to have them on what was supposed to be such a beautiful night."

Prudence swallowed hard and managed a weak nod before she rested her head back and closed her eyes once more. She tried not to, but more tears fell. Agnus squeezed her hand and encouraged her to rest her head on her shoulder again.

Thank goodness she did, too, because she spent the night adrift in crushing melancholy. Her deep sadness did not lessen over the next few weeks but seemed to worsen. She rarely ate or left her room. Letters were sent off to Maude and Emma that all was well, but she was capable of little more. Eventually, it seemed Agnus had had enough because she thrust the curtains open to blinding sunlight and placed a beautiful wooden box on her bed with Jacob's seal on it.

When Prudence shook her head, Agnus planted her hands on her hips. "I believe you made me a promise, my lady." She rested a cup of steaming tea on her bedside table and gestured at the box. "So either you start reading, or I will read them to you." One eyebrow crept up. "And I suspect you would rather I not do that."

She scowled. "You would not dare."

"I would." Agnus eyed her sternly. "And will if you do not."

It appeared she meant business because she sat down in a nearby chair, unwilling to leave. So Prudence could either read the letters or suffer her maid's hovering presence.

"Fine," she finally muttered, sitting up against the headboard. "If it means giving me peace and quiet again."

Agnus nodded once with approval as Prudence pulled the box closer. The idea of seeing Jacob's handwriting again and hearing his words, even if only on paper, was not as difficult as how she felt when she opened the sizeable box only to find it packed with unsent letters. Like her, he had written so many, seemingly only sending those he deemed most prevalent, and it broke her heart all over again.

Why had they not sent every letter? Had they feared it would be too much? They might drive the other away? Or perhaps it was the opposite, and they might pull them closer together? Either way, she had made Agnus a promise, so she started reading. Unlike their play on medieval times, the oldest ones were mainly more day-to-day in nature.

He envisioned walking her through his castle and telling her about its history. What she might think of his estate. As the letters went on, they became more personal in nature. He wondered what she would say to certain things. What advice she might give him. Questions that had more to do with matters of state. Letters that he could never risk traveling across Scotland and perhaps ending up in another's hands.

His correspondences had become more personal still as the months had rolled on. He'd envisioned her on his arm at events he hosted. Told her how seeing her across the room when he had to attend to business would make everything more bearable. They would exchange a knowing look and count down the minutes until they were alone again. Until he could hold her in his arms and make love to her.

She wiped away tears as she read letter after letter. Fenwick saw dinner brought up, and Agnus never left her side. As expected, Jacob's correspondence grew more passionate and intimate. Some recounted the hidden moments they had already shared, where others reflected on conversations they had enjoyed. Heated debates that ultimately landed them in bed.

It was one of the letters toward the end that caught her attention most, though.

One that touched on what she had overheard at MacLauchlin Castle before fleeing.

*19 February 1816*

*My Dearest Prudence,*

*I fear I have a confession to make. Something I should have told you sooner but was not sure how to voice it. You see, there was a time between you and my late wife that I was on a mission of sorts. One in which I was determined to save others as Elizabeth had saved me. Therefore, you should know there were lasses between you and Elizabeth. Not many. Just a few. I never laid with them nor found love, but I did find friendship and hope they felt the same.*

*I will tell you all of this when I arrive and apologize deeply for having been too spineless to tell you thus far. You deserve better, and I hope you will forgive me. More than that, I hope you will understand my motives.*

*All My Love,*
*Jacob*

Prudence lowered the letter and stared at it a moment. This had been right before they first made love. She recalled him speaking of how he had been before Elizabeth. How broken and callous because of his upbringing. How she had freed him from that terrible cage and made him a better person.

She continued on to the next letter.

*23 February 1816*

*My Dearest Heart, Prudence,*

*I cherished every moment we spent together at your new estate. You cannot know how much I have come to care for you. The love I suffer. The pain I felt when I left since we cannot be together every moment of every day.*

*Worse yet, I left without being truthful.*

*I never found the courage to confess about the lasses between you and Elizabeth. To that end, I am most certainly a coward. Why hesitate, you ask? Why hold back when you have every right to know? Because I fear, my love. Simple as that. I feared your response. Losing you. I cannot imagine not having you in my life. Never holding you again.*

*I will tell you next time we meet. It will be the first thing I do.*

*Yours Only,*
*Jacob*

"Yet you did not," she whispered.

"What, my lady?" Agnus said.

"I am not sure." She shook her head, not really seeing her maid when she looked at her but all the moments leading up to the here and now. From the letters she had received to the time spent with Jacob. "Other than to say I might have been a fool."

"I would think that quite impossible, my lady." Agnus sat beside her on the bed. Looked at her with unexpected wisdom.

"For foolish actions do not make a foolish person."

"I can only hope you are right, my friend," she whispered.

Agnus looked at her kindly and nodded. "I suspect I am." Her gaze went from the box to Prudence. "Shall you continue reading, or is all hope lost for your duke?"

"Lost?" She blinked back tears and reached for another letter. "I think perhaps not, after all."

Agnus smiled and nodded with approval before returning to her chair. Not to watch over her like a warrior of old standing guard on a battlement but as a friend, if she needed it.

Jacob had clearly struggled in letter upon unsent letter about whether he should tell her of his time after Elizabeth. He wanted no secrets between them. Yet ultimately, he had come to the conclusion it was best left behind them. He reiterated that he had not laid with those women, would never dishonor them like that, and they had gone on to good lives, so best he ended that chapter and started a new one with Prudence.

She closed her eyes and shook her head. What had she done? But she knew full well. She had let upper crust gossiping ladies rule her heart. Believed lies from strangers when she should have gone straight to her dearest friend and asked him for the truth. Because he would have given it to her. Just as he had in these letters. She had no doubt.

"I should have *never* fled that night." She blinked back more tears. "Had I just gone up there, he might have told—"

Her words were cut off by a rap at the door.

When she frowned at Agnus, her maid shrugged and went to the door only to find Fenwick on the other side. Pale as a ghost, he looked Prudence's way.

"What is it, Mr. Fenwick?" Agnus prompted when he seemed tongue-tied.

"This," he stammered, uncharacteristically shaken. He handed two letters to Agnus. "The Duke of Argyll has sent word. His driver waits below stairs lest you wish to speak with him."

Prudence went cold at the look on Fenwick's face before he

shut the door behind him. She and Agnus stared at each other for a moment before she did not bother reading the letters but swung out of bed. "Help me dress."

Agnus did and swiftly at that before Prudence flew downstairs to find Jacob's man standing in the foyer just as troubled as Fenwick.

"What is it?" Her voice shook. "What has happened?" Without doubt, something terrible. She knew it like she knew how to breathe. "Tell me now."

"My lady." The man bowed and did not quite look her in the eyes. "I come bearing sad news." He glanced from her servants to Prudence, clearly dreading his message. "News you may want to sit down for."

# Chapter Twenty

PRUDENCE STARED OUT Jacob's carriage window and saw nothing but leaden grey in what would normally be a glorious Scottish countryside. A world devoid of color as his carriage carried her south to what was left of him. Every second felt like years. The space between them infinite.

"My lady." Agnus tried to pry Jacob's latest letters out of her hand, but she only gripped the unopened envelopes more tightly. "Please, my friend." Her maid's voice softened. "Let me have them. Read them to you. The Duke of Argyll would have wanted that. It is why they were sent. Why they were rushed to you and you alone in his time of need."

"A time of need that has passed," she whispered hoarsely. "Because I was not there. Could not help him." Her vacant gaze dropped to his letters. "And now, these are all that are left of him."

"If so, then he thought highly of you indeed that he would see two letters delivered to you upon his death." Agnus shook her head. "Is that not strange?"

She choked back a sob and managed a weak shrug, unsure how to answer. Why *had* two letters been sent to her after Jacob suffered an accident? And such an accident. Evidently, a boar had charged his horse on a hunt. His mount had responded poorly and ended up crushing his arm. Soon after, an infection took root and ultimately ended his life.

"We now know he wrote me rather consistently," she said. "So is it so inconceivable two letters might be delivered at once?"

"It is when they had such specific instructions behind them," Agnus said.

Rather than respond, she closed her eyes and rested her head back against the seat. It seemed her friend would not take no for an answer, though, because she pried the letters out of her hands and gave her a look when she tried to retrieve them.

"I have been respectful up to this point, but that time has passed." Agnus arched her brows. "Unless, of course, you are willing to read the letters yourself?"

When she frowned, Agnus frowned as well. So either this would be a battle of wills or a surrender. Truth be told, she had little fight left in her, so she rested her head back again and closed her eyes, determined to tune out anything Agnus might say.

Something she failed miserably at when her maid read the first letter.

*14 July 1816*

*My Dearest Love,*

*I write this in the hopes you care to receive it. I have written you several times between watching your carriage pull away and now. Tried to make sense of what happened. Why you did not want me in the end. Because I can only assume that was your ultimate decision?*

*Why? What changed your mind? While desperate to know, I am afraid pride got in the way and kept me from reaching out sooner. I was hurt when you fled. Intensely so, if I am to be honest.*

*Now I lie here with a grave injury I am told will get better and see the error of my ways. In truth, I saw the error the moment my horse fell on me. Knew I should have gone to you sooner. Tried to understand why you fled when I swore you would join me on the battlements and say yes.*

*All aside, know I think of you now and hope our time*

*might not be over just yet.*

*Your Loving Jacob*

Prudence had no words. What had they done? Let pride and silliness get in the way of being together. Especially her. *Such foolishness.* When she gripped Agnus' wrist and nodded through tears, Agnus understood and opened the second letter.

*My Dearest Liege and Truest Love,*

*If you are reading this, then it seems I have succumbed to the battle and have been defeated. You should know my every thought has been with you since last we met to my dying breath. I fought to live so I could be by your side if you ever made your way back to me.*

*It seems despite one's best intentions, even the mightiest of warriors fall. Know this, though. You were my greatest love. The only one I will think of as I say goodbye to this life. Until next we meet…*

*Yours Always and Forever,*
*Jacob*

When Agnus stopped reading, she was every bit as teary as Prudence. Clearly just as heartbroken. Neither said another word, and she was grateful for it as she prayed for sleep to take her. Yet it only came in the form of Jacob. Only came with him standing on the battlements, awaiting her.

Every minute, be it waking or sleeping was awful. Like a waking nightmare until the carriage slowed, then stopped. She looked at Agnus, terrified. How was she supposed to do this? How was she supposed to see him this way?

Where she thought the door would open to a somber footman dressed in mourning clothes, instead, Emma opened the door and breathed a sigh of relief when she saw Prudence.

"Thank the good Lord." She pulled Prudence after her. "Come. Please. Straight away, as I am sure you will make all the difference."

What possible difference could she make now?

"How?" A door opened for them at the top of the castle stairs. "I do not understand. Is everyone not in mourning? I was told Jacob had passed. That he—"

"Passed?" Emma frowned and led her up more stairs inside. "Not yet, and by the grace of God, not for many years to come."

Daring not to hope, Prudence shook her head. "Then why was I told otherwise?"

"Because, at the time, we thought him lost to us, Lady Barrington." Mr. Donal fell in step beside her with a furrowed brow as Emma rushed her down a hallway. "When I sent our man to retrieve you, we thought his Grace had succumbed to illness, but miraculously he pulled through, if but barely. Suffice it to say, you received his last two letters. Correspondences suited to each possible outcome as it were."

When they reached a large, ornate door, Emma finally slowed, looked at Prudence, and pleaded with her eyes.

"If anyone can keep him with us, it is you, dear Lady Barrington." She blinked back tears and explained how Jacob's fever had not lessened any, nor had he woken in days.

"Why me?" She struggled to find her voice. Tried to grasp what they were telling her. Jacob was still alive? He had not left her yet?

"Because I believe you have kept him alive thus far," Mr. Donal said softly. He opened Jacob's bedroom door and gestured at the sizeable box at his bedside. The one in which she had put her own unsent letters. A box Agnus must have provided him.

"I hope you do not mind, but I read them to him the moment he began fighting fever and would no longer open his eyes," Emma said. "He mumbled your name often, so I suspect they kept him with us somehow."

Of course, she did not mind. Anything to keep him here. She went to Jacob, cupped his fevered cheek, and bit back tears. "I will stay with him. Read more to him." She spoke to anyone listening.

"Get me a cold cloth straight away."

After that, she was aware of little else but Jacob over the next few days. She pressed a cool cloth against his hot forehead. Read the remaining letters she meant to send but never did.

Much like his correspondence, they spoke of day-to-day things she thought he might find trivial. Then others, further along, talked of fearing her love for him. The last letter was more poignant than the rest. She could hardly believe Agnus had handed it over but knew she had to read it. Jacob needed to hear what she had written right before heading to MacLauchlin Castle.

So she took his hand and read.

*22 June 1816*

*My Dearest Love,*

*I have been debating for days whether I should go to the MacLauchlin's Midsummer Ball because I fear how to respond to you. A fear like you cannot imagine. Why, you ask? Quite simply. What if I say yes and become caged again by marriage? Or so I thought that was my singular fear.*

*You see, in the end, I realized there was more to my hesitation.*

*Rather, it occurred to me my greatest fear was losing who I had become over the past several months. I once affiliated marriage with the loss of who I had once been. What it turned me into thereafter. Worried that somehow, someway, I would become that hardened, cruel woman again if I ever remarried.*

*Yet with the revelation of my greatest fear came peace and certainty. Not only because I would never allow myself to go there again but because you, my love, would see that woman freed if she ever dared return.*

She laid down beside him and rested her cheek on his chest. Willed his heartbeat to get stronger as she continued reading.

*So now I ready myself to come to you at MacLauchlin Castle, where you can rest assured, I will be counting down the*

*minutes until I join you on our battlements. Those precious*
*moments when I say yes, my dear duke, I will become your wife.*
*I only hate I waited so long to say so, my love.*

She set aside the letter and spoke close to his ear so he might
hear her clearly. "Yes, Jacob, I will marry you. Over and over,
time and time again, so come back to me. *Stay* with me."

While she liked to believe he stirred, when she looked at his
face, he remained still. And he continued to stay that way for days
on end. Days during which she rarely left his side. She cared
naught what people thought. Not in the least.

The only time she left was to bathe, after which she allowed
Emma to give her brief tours of the castle so she might tell Jacob
what she thought. How she envisioned him showing her around,
instead. From the armory hall with its twenty-one-meter-tall
ceilings and more weapons than one could count to its exquisite
state dining room. She was shown the stunning Parisian-style
tapestry drawing room and the saloon with its grand pianoforte.
Afterward, she would chat with him about the discussions they
might have. Which parts of the castle she suspected he liked best.
Which parts she favored over others.

She also commented on the touching paintings in his bedroom. Ones that warmed her heart and told her so much. How
could they not, considering how familiar they were? While not
exact replicas for obvious reasons, one depicted a torch-lit
battlement with a couple embracing in the shadows. Another, of
the same shadowed couple sitting in a study by a crackling fire.
The third of the couple picnicking in a sunlit oasis nestled in the
woodland.

Prudence knew nothing about nursing but learned. Made it
her mission. Trickled water and cooled soup down Jacob's throat.
He would not like her seeing to more private matters, so she left
that to others but always returned to his side afterward. She read
to him late into the night and kept him abreast of castle happenings to the best of her ability.

"Will he lose his arm?" she asked the doctor almost a week later. "Or is it healing?"

Emma made it clear the doctor should answer any questions Prudence might have. She was considered next of kin. To that end, the doctor responded after examining him and was more hopeful than either of them expected.

"I would have thought it unlikely a week ago," the doctor confessed. "But now, I think otherwise. The skin is healing. Color is beginning to return." He looked from Emma to Prudence. "While I cannot speak to him waking again, I dare say there is reason for hope now. Reason I thought lost to us."

After she and Emma glanced at each other with much-needed optimism, Prudence resumed sitting by his side. Chatted about anything she could think of. Her estate and their time there. Moments yet to come. Then more about his castle and their years ahead there, too. How beautiful it was with its sweeping Gothic Revival architecture and vibrant gardens. How proud he should be that he was its laird, as they said here in Scotland. From what she had heard, he had been an excellent laird thus far too. A truly admirable duke.

Keeping that in mind, she spoke of all the good things he had done and all they might do going forward together. How he might take her to surrounding towns so she could get to know his people better. *Their* people. How they would continue resurrecting Scotland with not just his time and money but hers as well. How they might also find a way to create more jobs. Commerce and opportunity. Help those in need, as she knew that weighed on his mind.

As she did every night, she crawled into bed beside him and held him. Pressed cool compresses against him. Willed him back to her. It was on the eighth night, though, that she felt confident enough to do something she had not done thus far.

Something she prayed finally brought him back to her.

# Chapter Twenty-One

CRESTFALLEN OVER PRUDENCE'S rejection, Jacob had left the MacLauchlin's Midsummer Ball that very night, eager to get home. Or should he say desperate to get anywhere that allowed him time alone. Away from anything that reminded him of her. Clear of the heartache and terrible sense of loss he felt when he watched her carriage pull away.

To his mind, that meant returning to his castle, where there were no reminders of her. Although he went about business as usual, his days felt empty and hollow. Lacked meaning and purpose. Yet he knew his people needed him, so he set aside his anger and grief. Set aside emotions that could not be shown around his castle.

He could show them beyond it, though.

Especially when he went hunting one warm, blustery day. He had been pursuing a boar and pushed his horse too hard. So he could not be angered when the boar turned on them, and his horse reared. Could not be upset when the boar was shot down, but not before his horse fell and landed on his arm.

He recalled his horse's cry. Felt excruciating pain. The next thing he remembered, he was on the ground, covered in blood. His last thoughts were of how foolish and impulsive he had been.

Was his horse all right? He hoped he did not suffer.

"Your horse is just fine, Your Grace," he swore someone said but could not be sure through his pain.

For that matter, he could not be sure of much after that.

Was he back in his castle or at Prudence's estate? Because he swore she was there comforting him with her cool, soothing touch. That she read to him. Shared letters he had never heard before.

At several points, he tried to respond but could not.

Rather, he continued listening. When her letters ended, she talked of his estate. How she'd toured it without him and had much to say, so best he listen. He imagined that he walked with her. Conversed with her. Discussed everything he showed her. As always, she was inquisitive. And, as always, he was enchanted by her. Loved that she had finally come. That he could, at last, escort her through his corridors. Show her his hallways full of old paintings.

Every so often, he would pull her close and kiss her. Tell her he was crestfallen she had decided not to be with him in the end. How sorry he was that he kept the truth from her about the lasses he had helped after his wife died. He hoped she understood he meant no harm. Those relationships had paled in comparison to what he shared with her.

How he felt about her.

"You say all this," she whispered into his mind. "Yet you lie there when I know you have more to say. Know you want to come back to me."

Come back to her? *She* had left him. Fled without telling him why. Better still, fled, telling him everything he needed to know. Or so it had seemed despite feeling her by his side even now.

He had watched her carriage pull away. *Knew* she was gone.

Even so, she continued to whisper in his ear. Told him how much she loved him. How she had every intention of marrying him. He had it all wrong. She had joined him on the battlements.

Run into his arms.

Kissed him.

Agreed to marry him.

"You have to stay with me, my love," she murmured, yet again making no sense. She placed his hand over warmth. "You have to stay with *us*."

Something about that. The urgency in her voice, combined with the heat beneath his fingertips, made everything suddenly seem different. Closer. Part of him in a way that made things crisper. Brighter.

So bright he opened his eyes and blinked.

"Prudence," he said hoarsely, parched. "Are you there, lass?"

"I am." Her face appeared above him, her smile warm. She cupped his cheek. "Welcome back, love."

Never so happy to see her, he tried to respond, but it was too difficult.

"No, no." Prudence put a finger to his lips. "You have been ill for some time, but you are back with me now. Back with us." She narrowed her eyes, challenging him to defy her. "And by us, I mean me and the babe in my womb, so you best stay right where you are and *never* think of leaving again."

He could do little more than try to smile as she faded into darkness. Eventually, light returned, and he opened his eyes again. Terrified he had lost her once more, he bolted upright, only for his doctor to ease him back down.

"Rest, my love." Prudence sat beside him and gazed at him lovingly. "Rest so we can marry the moment you are well."

"Post the banns," he managed, grateful for the cup of water the doctor brought to his lips. "Do not hesitate."

"I will not."

"She did not," Emma corrected, sitting on his other side when the doctor stepped away. She took his hand and smiled. "Welcome back, dear friend."

He gazed around the room, trying to take stock of his surroundings before he recalled what had happened with vivid clarity. How his horse had crushed his arm.

Alarmed, he frowned at Emma. "Tell me they did not hurt my horse. That—"

"Your horse is just fine." She gestured at his wounded arm. "As is your arm, thank the good Lord."

He breathed a sigh of relief over his horse before his gaze flew back to Prudence. Had he heard what he thought he heard, or had it been a dream? A mere fantasy?

"Tell me," he whispered, praying she knew of that which he spoke. That he had not been delirious.

"I will leave you two alone," Emma murmured, fading into the background.

"Tell me, my love." He needed to know if what had seemed the impossible happened. "Did you…are you…"

"I am." Prudence rested her hand over her womb. "I have not bled since we lay together in our sun-dappled woodland oasis." Her eyes grew glassy. "Your doctor has confirmed I am with child."

He fought back pure joy. Worried for her. "How do you feel? Should you not rest?"

"I feel fine," Prudence said. "Much better than I did when I thought I lost you." She squeezed his hand. Gazed into his eyes with the same love he felt for her. "Now I burst with happiness. I cannot begin to tell you how overjoyed I am that you are well. That we might finally start our life together."

Having never heard sweeter words, he urged her to crawl beneath the blankets and lay beside him so he might hold her. When she did, they held each other for a while before inevitably making sense of things.

She explained why she had not joined him on the battlements before eventually reading his unsent letters. He explained his fear of losing her if he told her the truth. Both vowed to voice their fears straight away in the future and never keep secrets from one another again.

They also recognized and felt fortunate for their servants' roles in ultimately keeping them together.

"So how fares Mr. Donal and Miss Agnus now?" he wondered.

"In the end, peace was found on the battlefield, dear second-in-command." Prudence grinned at him. "Peace, I think we can both agree, made all the difference for us." She winked. "For them, too, by the sounds of it."

He met her smile. "Then we shall see them well wed, indeed."

"Indeed," she echoed.

While he could not make love to Prudence quite yet, he longed for the moment he could because he intended to cherish her heart and flesh until the very end. Counted his blessings that they had found each other when it had seemed so improbable they would. Not like this.

Never so intensely nor true.

So it was the Duke of Argyll, and Lady Barrington married a few short weeks later. Their wedding was small but well received, their deep love plain for all to see. As was the love they felt for their baby boy when he arrived in January of the following year.

A child who was the first of several bairns as their love flourished over the years.

Love that proved far more sustaining than any could have imagined, given how they had begun. But then, as he told her time and time again, it was only ever a matter of trusting their love once they united. More than that, never second-guessing a lord when he knew they should always be together.

## THE END

Interested in following Blake and Maude's love story? Look for *Harrowing Hall*, A Second-time Brides spin-off. Eager to roll back the clock further and lose yourself in the medieval Scottish romances that ultimately resurrected Castle MacLauchlin nearly five hundred years ago? Join Laird Teagan MacLauchlin and his brothers in Sky Purington's *Highlander's Pact* series.

# About the Author

Sky Purington is the bestselling author of over fifty novels and novellas. A New Englander born and bred who recently moved to Virginia, Purington married her hero, has an amazing son who inspires her daily and two ultra-lovable husky shepherd mixes. Passionate for variety, Sky's vivid imagination spans several romance genres, including historical, time travel, paranormal, and fantasy. Expect steamy stories teeming with protective alpha heroes and strong-minded heroines.

Purington loves to hear from readers and can be contacted at Sky@SkyPurington.com. Interested in keeping up with Sky's latest news and releases? Either visit Sky's website, www.SkyPurington.com, join her quarterly newsletter, or sign up for personalized text message alerts. Simply text 'skypurington' (no quotes, one word, all lowercase) to 74121 or visit Sky's Sign-up Page. Texts will ONLY be sent when there is a new book release. Readers can easily opt out at any time.

Love social networking? Find Sky on Facebook, Instagram, Twitter, and Goodreads.

Want a few more options? "Follow" Sky Purington on Amazon to receive New Release Kindle Updates and "Follow" Sky on BookBub to be notified of amazing upcoming deals.